The Family Stone

Debbie R. Reynolds

The Family Stone

ISBN 978-0-578-63372-5

Cover design by Marion Designs

Three Sons' Press

Chapter 1

Kim glanced around, still amazed at the room she now shared with Andrea. It was like something on the television show, "My Super Sweet Sixteen."
She had been through so much, and now that this new family had asked her to spend the summer with them, she hoped her life would settle down for a while.

What have I done to deserve this, she wondered? Then she smiled and climbed out of bed to face the morning.

Peering out the window on her side of the room, the hills and mountains were endless, just like the direction of her new life.

The sun even looked different in California. She closed her eyes, allowing the sun to warm her from the outside in. It had been two days since her arrival in San Diego, and everything still seemed unreal—the beautiful mountains, the house, instant family, and the plan to go to high school here. She hoped to do well enough in high school to get accepted into UCLA for college.

Kim opened her tattered suitcase and looked for something nice to wear. It was a big day. Her dresser was being delivered and she was going with Andrea (and Andrea's mother, Allison) to spend a girls' day out. Allison's sons: Kevin, Mark, and Julian, were happy to stay behind with their father, Robert, to do yard work and take stuff to the dump.

Kevin and Mark could have passed for twins, taking the narrow jaw line from their dad. The only difference was Kevin had his mother's complexion. Julian resembled his sister, same height even; barely above the height necessary to ride roller coasters.

Kim hoped that it wouldn't take long before she felt at home with her adopted family. Her suitcase and clothing seemed out of place in the perfect bedroom. There wasn't much to choose from, but she settled on a pair of faded pink sweatpants and a white t-shirt—one of the few outfits still intact. Kim then slid the suitcase back under the bed, leaving most of her clothes just where she had packed them back in Omaha, Texas.

Andrea had practice for her high school dance team, but Allison promised to take the girls to lunch afterwards and then do a little shopping.

Waiting for Andrea's practice to end was the first time Kim would be alone with Allison. Everything was strange and foreign. She wished Kevin would go with them, even though he told her not to worry.

She felt her stomach rumbling with nervous energy. The rural town where she had lived her whole life until then was so tiny and San Diego was huge.

Kim wondered if she would fit in or be an outsider. Everyone felt compassion and love for adopted babies, but teenagers were in a class by themselves.

Kim's life changed overnight after her mother, Maggie, died of breast cancer. There was no one to help her with homework. The person who was charged with explaining all the changes to her body was gone. It was like a horror movie with Kim, the main character, watching her life fall apart in slow motion.

Her father, Francis, found his solace in the bottom of a bottle. Drinking replaced everything else in his life.

A month before she left Texas, a teenager shot Francis right out front of their house. She came home to an empty house splattered with blood stains. While she stood in the living room shivering with pools of tears forming in her eyes, Francis was at the hospital fighting for his life. Although Francis recovered from the shooting incident, Kim felt like she had lost her family and everything that was important to her. Francis loved his daughter, but he was not able to pull it together after her mother's death. Drinking heavily and running a family was like mixing oil and water.

Having escaped the unrest and turmoil of that life, Kim was aware that the new family didn't have to keep her. The generosity of Kevin's family could end at any time. Kevin was their biological son, but Kim had no blood ties to any of them. She could get thrown back to that awful life in tiny Omaha as easily as fishermen tossed unwanted fish back into lakes. Better to stay under the radar, and keep any requests to a minimum.

Kim finished getting ready. She washed her face, brushed her teeth, and then headed to the kitchen for breakfast. A plate was on the stove, covered with a napkin with a note on top.

Kim, here is your breakfast. We will see you around 10:30

The scrambled eggs, bacon, smothered potatoes with grilled onions, and biscuit stared back at her. She ate until her stomach was full, quietly savoring every bite. Besides, she had to eat everything; it was impolite to waste food.

Kim noticed the dishwasher, but thought it would be better to clean her plate and put it away. She would rather not have anything she used left out to be noticed.

The echoes in the empty house mirrored the way her heart felt. She walked outside to sit on the patio in the sun. Her thoughts wandered back to Texas. Her dad was alone.

Leaving the life she knew for the unknown had been hard for Kim and Francis. Kim made the decision to leave him, and now she was worried. How would he survive without her? He was still healing from the shooting. Was she wrong for abandoning him when he needed her the most?

Guilt gripped Kim's face. Families stayed together and weathered the storms. She did not want her father to hate her.

Francis was released from the hospital the day Kim left for San Diego. Instead of being there for him, she left a letter explaining her decision to start a new life away from him. She knew that abandoning someone who loved her for a family she didn't know might be a crazy thing to do, but she believed that life had to be better elsewhere. It had to be.

Kim heard a car pull up in the driveway, and that broke her daydreaming. She went inside to see if it was time to leave.

"Mom's waiting in the car!" Andrea yelled as she bounced down the hallway. "I am going to

5

change and I will be out."

"Okay," Kim replied.

Andrea was back in less than a minute, clothes crisp, wearing a pink tank top, pink flip-flops, and white jean shorts too revealing for a girl her age. As she passed Kim to go out the front door, she said, "Don't leave your shoes in the middle of the floor. For now, they can go under your bed. I will clear a little space for you when we get back."

"Sorry," Kim replied, as she followed Andrea out the front door. Technically, six inches from her bed didn't exactly add up to the middle of the floor, but Kim recognized a need for diplomacy and remained quiet.

"Hello, Kim good morning!" Allison said cheerfully. "I hoped you enjoyed breakfast. Robert made it."

"It was great, thank you," Kim replied.

"I thought we could go to the mall. I am sure we can find some things you like there." Allison said.

Kim cleared her throat. "That sounds great."

"First, I want to go to H&M and then Macy's," Andrea said. "There is this skirt I want. Then we can get the swimsuit I've been looking at."

"That sounds good," Allison answered.

Kim listened to the conversation from the back seat, envious of the closeness between Andrea and Allison. They laughed and joked with each other easily.

Allison smelled like honeysuckle, sweet and calming, and her voice drew you into her conversation. That must be what it felt like to have a mother in your life, Kim thought. She remembered the time spent with her mother, Maggie. Those were her best memories, and she missed that time very much.

"Kim, what stores would you like to go to?"

Allison asked, looking at her through the rearview mirror.

"I am sure I will find something wherever we go. I've never been to a mall before."

"Well, then you will enjoy Plaza Bonita." Allison said.

Allison drove into the parking lot near the Macy's entrance. Kim stared at the huge store. She hadn't had new clothes since Francis confiscated the inheritance money they received after their mother died. There had been happiness in their house at that time. While her father had money, he had bought her new clothes and paid for her cheerleading uniform. Life had been pleasant for that short period of time.

"We'll park by Macy's since we're gonna end our shopping there," Allison said. "Let's hit the mall. I love shopping!"

They headed for H&M. The store was filled with so many clothes. "Too many choices," Kim mumbled as she went to the dressing room to try on a couple of short, animal-print sundresses.

Kim looked in the mirror, and frowned at the skeletal reflection, with tired eyes that stared back at her. She saw the pain she had been through during the months since Kevin left her in Texas. It was hard to be excited about shopping. Most of the sundresses fit too loosely, like a grandmother's dress. Then the black one, a fitted knit dress that barely covered her butt, made her feel self-conscious. She handed the dresses back to the clerk.

"Did you find anything?" Allison asked.

"Not yet."

"Don't worry, Kim. I am sure we will have better luck at Macy's. Let me pay for Andrea's skirts and we can go over there now."

Walking down the white-pillared walkway between the stores, there were so many stores. She whipped her head around taking in everything. There were accessories, lotions, and little stands selling hair products and toy airplanes. There was even a movie theatre located inside the mall.

Kim bumped into a group of kids watching a demonstration. "Excuse me," she said, embarrassed by her lapse.

"What is a Hot dog on a stick?" Kim said.

It made her mouth water, but it would be impolite to ask for food when Allison had already been nice enough to take her shopping. Kim took one last look at the frying corn dogs and swallowed her words.

"We will get you a few outfits, a pair of pj's, and a swimsuit," Allison announced as they entered Macy's.

Allison was beautiful, like Vanessa Williams, with short-cropped hair and a chocolate smooth complexion.

"Do you like these?" she asked Kim, while picking out a pair of pj's that were pink with purple polka dots.

"Yes," Kim answered.

Allison smiled. "Oh good."

They moved onto swimsuits. Kim picked out a two-piece tankini and a one-piece blue strapless suit. Allison let her keep both.

The outfits were harder to choose. Kim would have worn sweats every day, but it was summer and it was too hot to wear what felt familiar to her. She allowed Allison to pick out the clothing. It seemed like the smart thing, considering she did not have the faintest fashion sense on what was proper California attire.

As they shopped, Kim noticed that Andrea seemed bored. Whenever Allison spoke to Kim, Andrea crossed her arms and twisted her body so that her back was facing them. But even when she was pouting, Andrea was pretty. She looked like a young version of her mother, down to the light-brown, teddy-bear eyes, with long eyelashes. She had worn her hair flat-ironed bone-straight. It fell down her back in an A-line cut. She was too cute to act so ugly.

"Can I have a new bikini?" Andrea asked.

"You got a new one two days ago and one last week," her mother replied. "Pick out something else."

Andrea stomped away. Kim watched her, each step calculated, screaming that the discussion was not over.

Kim gathered her bags. They swayed as they walked toward the door. "Thank you," Kim said.

"You are welcome. Andrea, come on. We're going to get some lemonade."

Andrea walked two feet behind her mother, throwing daggers with her eyes. "I am not thirsty."

"Kim, you want to try a corn dog? They really are delicious."

Kim's eyes widened and she perked up. She felt her mouthwatering again. "Sure, I'll try one."

They ate in silence.

Kim's dresser had been delivered, by the time they arrived home. She had a place for her clothes in the battered suitcase, including a few dresses Maggie had lovingly made for her. No matter how out of style they were, Kim could not part with them. They were a part of her and she was not willing to lose anything else.

Kim noticed Andrea untying a bikini top from under her t-shirt and slipping out of the bikini bottoms under her shorts. Her mouth fell open.

"Mind your own business," Andrea spat out. "Keep your mouth shut and you might survive the summer."

It was the pink with white polka dots

9

swimsuit Andrea had asked her mother to buy when they were shopping at the mall. Kim could see that Andrea was a girl used to getting her way, by any means necessary.

Chapter 2

Kim had been in San Diego for a week now, and everything still seemed foreign. Nervous and uneasy about her place in this family, she walked on eggshells around the house; hoping to fit in and not be noticed at the same time.

Andrea's attitude had been cold toward Kim, and nothing seemed to thaw her behavior. But Kim would not be bullied by anyone, especially when it was unjustified. She decided to try to smooth things over.

That night while they were lying in bed, Kim gathered her bravery and asked in a clear, loud voice, "Can we try to be friends, Andrea?"

"Not interested," Andrea replied immediately.

"Well, are you willing to try and get along?"

"Look, no one asked my permission for you

to invade my space; therefore, I don't have to try anything."

"I've done nothing to you. I had hoped to at least get to know you, but I see you have already made up your mind. So, I'll try to stay out of your way. The rules toward sharing were taught in kindergarten. You must've missed the lesson?" Kim clinched her fist under her blanket.

"Just stay out of my way and leave my things alone. Trust, I will report any theft to the police."

"Maybe you should report yourself first, for that swimsuit," Kim slung back at her. "Shoot, if that's how you wanna play it, don't think I forgot."

"Whatever, I have money. I don't need to steal. You just keep your nose in your own business and let me handle mine." Andrea rolled her eyes and slammed the door.

Kim turned over in bed. She felt like screaming, but it would not help. It was only one week in and she was already having problems with Andrea—who was turning out to be a witch. Andrea had everything she wanted and did not appreciate any of it.

Kim and her mother Maggie never had much and there were many times when she had no food or clothes in Texas. But they would rather starve or wear the same tattered clothes every day than to take something that was not theirs. No matter how down and out they were – even when Kim's father spent all their money on gambling and alcohol – Kim never stole anything. It broke a code of honor that Maggie had instilled in her. So, she could not understand why anyone would steal, especially when they had the money. It was plain stupid.

Kim felt like she had done her part by trying to become friends. What more could she do? How could she get along with someone who was so self-centered? How would Kim live in a room with someone who hated her existence?

Andrea and Kim's bedroom felt like a cubbyhole. It had been four days since their confrontation, but they managed to stay out of each other's way.

Andrea finally spoke to Kim on the fifth day after the argument.

"Family meeting at the dinner table at seven," Andrea announced, as she walked out of the room.

"Okay," Kim mumbled toward the closing door.

Kim thought a lot about her dad: Was he capable of supporting himself since she was gone? Had he healed from the shooting well enough to go find work? Were the delinquents who shot him rotting in jail? She missed him. Being without him hurt a lot because she knew he would be the perfect father if it weren't for alcohol.

Nevertheless, Kim knew she could not go back and live with Francis. Not for a while anyway. Her big concern for the time being was getting along with Andrea. And if she didn't get along with Andrea, how long would the family allow her to stay?

Kim envied Kevin, who seemed to have acclimated into the family seamlessly. He worked at the local movie theatre during the summer, so he was rarely home. He did come by her room every night to talk about his day and to ask how she was doing. Just the previous night, they talked about old times.

"Remember the day we spent sitting in the car all day, waiting on Francis to come out of that card room?" Kevin asked.

Kim laughed. "Yeah, it was so hot that day. But that bar-be-que was delicious."

"Yeah, under any other circumstances, I would have loved it. He made me so mad the way he treated us. I don't think I could ever forgive him,

Kim."

"He was wrong. I'm not saying he wasn't. But we must forgive people. Kevin, he's been your father for sixteen years. He could use forgiveness," she nearly pleaded with her brother.

"He was not my father. He turned his back completely on us. He did so many things wrong. I don't know if I can just let it go. Living out here has showed me how much we missed out on in Texas. I have a future here. I am going to college next year."

"That's great. I am happy for you," Kim replied. "I'm just saying."

"Yeah, I know."

They stay silently for a few moments.

"Kevin," Kim began again, "I'm sorry I didn't believe you about Dad's drinking. You were right."

"He is not my dad," Kevin answered in a low tone. "I'm living with my real dad, but you're right, Francis definitely has a problem. Only, we don't have to worry about him anymore. Dad will take care of us now. You have a home here with us."

Kim looked at Kevin. He was right. Robert was his dad, but not her father. What had she done coming here? How would Kevin's family ever accept her? She was not their biological daughter, and they did not have to keep her or love her. This was not her home. She was a stranger, trying to fit in. Kim frowned, and stared at the speck of lint on the floor.

"You will fit in," Kevin reassured her. "Give it time."

"I don't think Andrea likes me. What can I do?"

"She is cool. She just needs to get to know you and you guys will be okay. Give her some time."

Kim didn't believe it would be that easy. Andrea didn't seem like the type of person who warmed up to anyone, especially an outsider who was taking up space in her room without her permission. This was going to be a very hard adjustment and Kevin had no clue.

Kim tensed her shoulders and looked at her brother. "Well, I hope you're right. Hey, can we catch a movie this weekend?"

"Rain check. I got a date with my girl, Grace," Kevin answered with a big gin. "But don't worry. We will have time. Hey, I gotta grab a shower and get some sleep. We will talk tomorrow."

"Is she your girlfriend?" Kim asked.

"Yes, we have only been going out for a few weeks now. If things work out, you will meet her," Kevin answered, as he walked down the hallway.

Kim had mixed feelings about her debriefing with Kevin. She felt a distance growing between them that was never there before. Now that he had real parents and a girlfriend, things felt different. Kim didn't even tell him about the confrontation she had with Andrea. But maybe he was right; maybe she and Andrea just needed more time to mesh. After all, she was invading Andrea's space. She would be patient and give her new sister some time.

The door to the room opened again and Andrea entered talking on her cell phone. She ended her call and docked her iPod. The speakers flooded the room with Trey Song's, "Bottoms Up," shattering Kim back into realty.

Kim looked over at Andrea dancing in the mirror and brushing her hair. Kim was invisible to her. With Kevin's advice still on her mind, she said nothing and crossed her fingers that Andrea would come around soon.

Instead, she decided to get out of the house for some fresh air. Kim had enjoyed running since she had run track for the school in Texas. It always helped clear her head. She had enough time to go for a quick run before dinner, so she changed into her grey sweats and pink tennis shoes, grabbed her sneakers, and headed out of her bedroom and towards the front door. She was not sure of the protocol for leaving the house alone, so she made sure she checked first.

"Allison," Kim asked with a weak smile. "I would like to go for a run around our block before dinner, if that's okay?"

"Yes, go ahead, be careful, stay on the sidewalk," Allison replied. "Dinner will be ready in one hour and we have the family meeting right after dinner."

Kim nodded firmly. "I'll be back in time."

Running was a great way to learn the neighborhood, Kim figured. She would ask Robert if she could call Francis after the family meeting.

Running easily down Noeline Way as it sloped gradually downhill leading to the steeper windy Noeline Avenue, which challenged Kim's endurance and breathing while jogging to the top of the hill. Neighbors waved as she passed their houses. Kim smiled and waved back. The air was clean and refreshing and was helping her focus. She thought about her dad, Francis. Kevin still seemed so mad at him, and for good reason. But Francis had a kind heart and Kim knew he loved her. That is why she could not be angrier with him; she felt too sorry for him to hold onto much anger.

This new family could dump her whenever they felt like it; there was no telling when their kindness might run out. This was a scary feeling. She had heard stories about teens living on the street and Kim did not want to be one of those teens. She began to rethink ever-leaving Texas.

She continued running, and slowly her life in

Texas came rushing back to her. They lived in a house without electricity and water. There was hardly food to eat, and Francis often brought drunken men home with him. Sometimes it seemed like she might do better living on the street since her dad did not mind bringing the streets into their home.

As she ran, Kim thought about Keith and Tim, two great friends she left behind. Keith, her 6'1" knight in shining armor, taught her a great deal about boys. He came along after Kevin left and saved her the night she found out about her father being shot.

Tim was her next-door neighbor and pseudo brother. She imaged him practicing summer football like always and breaking some new girl's heart. It made her smile to think about the fellows. She missed them.

Sweat dripped down Kim's forehead as she jogged up Noeline Avenue. By the time she reached the crest of the hill, her legs started to burn. She stopped at the top and bent over to stretch her muscles, then turned around and headed back down the hill. As she jogged down the street toward her new temporary home, she realized she still wanted to talk to her father back in Texas. She needed to be sure he was doing all right.

She headed back up the street feeling a little uneasy about how to reenter the house. She never knew what to say. She couldn't shake her anxiety.

When she walked in, Allison was setting the table for dinner.

"You need some help?" Kim asked.

"I got it, sweetie," Allison answered without looking up. "You go get cleaned up. Dinner will be ready soon."

Kim went into the bathroom to take a quick shower before dinner. The meal was uneventful and no one seemed concerned about the family meeting

Andrea had mentioned earlier.

"Kim how was your first week?" Robert asked.

"Nice," Kim said simply.

"Well, I want to go over our family rules, so you'll know how we do things here," Robert responded. "I should've done this right when you arrived."

Kim shifted in her seat. "Okay."

"All of our kids have a curfew of eleven, so we expect you home by that time too. All the kids have chores that revolve each week. Allison made a chart that we will hang up in the kitchen," Robert explained.

"We want you to be a part of our family as long as you are here," Allison added, "and being a part means participating. Can you handle that?"

All eyes turned to Kim. What could she say? It sounded reasonable. She remembered her mother Maggie had rules too, like homework first and then you could play outside. You had to be in the house before dark. Maggie insisted on the whole family eating dinner together. And Kim remembered taking out the trash, cleaning her room, and Kevin doing the dishes. But after Maggie's death, Francis's alcohol problems worsened and rules seemed to fade away. Suddenly, Kevin became the family cook, and no one cared when they ate, slept, or whether they got up for school on time. It would be a challenge for Kim to adapt to rules again because when she was used to policing herself.

What could she expect of Robert and Allison? Would they disappoint her like her dad? Adults were not always reliable. So far, these two adults had been fair. Kevin had spent a year with them and he trusted them. He was a hard critic, so maybe it would be okay for her to trust them too, at least a little bit.

"That sounds fair," Kim said, managing a small smile.

"If you need anything, ask. We will make sure you have what you need. Here is a list of activities at the local recreation center. We thought you would enjoy finding something to do for the summer," Allison responded.

Kim was shocked. Nobody had ever offered her summer activities before. She had always just stayed at home while her parents worked. This was all new to her. "Thanks, I will look it over."

Robert looked at his wife and then back at Kim. "Do you have any questions for us?"

"Is that all you expect from me?" Kim asked.

"Yes, we want you to be a kid again and enjoy it. We'll treat you just like the rest of our kids, "Robert replied. "Anyone else have anything to discuss?"

"No," the other kids replied in unison.

Kim wanted to ask about calling her dad, but she didn't want to seem ungrateful.

"Oh, one more thing, Kim, all of the kids have cell phones. We got you one too," Robert said.

Kim's eyes lit up like a Christmas tree when she saw the pink iPhone in Robert's hand.

"Thank you!"

"You have unlimited calls and unlimited text messages. You can call your Dad if you want to," Robert informed her, as he handed over the phone. "Meeting over."

Kim held the phone to her chest, smiling. The meeting had gone well; it felt good to have a clear understanding of their expectations. They even gave her a phone. She had never had one before. She could call her friends and her dad finally.

Her father didn't have a phone at their house, so she would have to call Tim's house, which was right next door. But what if her Dad refused to come to the phone; she went back and forth in her head. She had to try and talk to him. She walked to her room and sat on her bed. Her heart sped up as she dialed the number. It rang eight times and went to voicemail. Kim left her new number and said she could be reached after five Texas time.

She waited all night for a call back. When she finally went to sleep, her new phone rested on her pillow. She would try to call tomorrow.

Chapter 3

When Kim opened her eyes the next morning, the pink cell phone stared back at her. To her, this was the best thing since ice cream. This tiny devise held a great deal of responsibility and Kevin's parents had put trust in her to uphold their rules. She would not let them down. Except for Andrea, the family all seemed to be welcoming her into the fold.

Kim jumped out of bed, rushing through the shower to be on time for her first summer activity: a dance class at the recreation center. Once she was dressed, she stuffed the phone into her pocket, grabbed her borrowed black nylon backpack, and stuffed a bottle of water and a towel into it. On the kitchen table, she found a note from Allison: Here is the fee for your class and your house key. See you tonight!

Remembering her previous run, Kim turned left out of the driveway, down the hill at a slow jog. There was a pleasant breeze blowing in her face as she reached the crest of the hill. She crossed the street and continued through the park until she got to the rec center.

A group of girls gathered near the entrance signing in on a roster sheet. Kim got in line behind them. She tried to hide her excitement. When her turn came, she signed her name and gave the teacher her check. The teacher handed her back a permission slip that had to be signed and brought back. It was the most normal teenager experience she'd had in a long while.

Suddenly, Kim felt a little nervous and nauseous. She had never taken dance before. She moved to the rear of the class, placed her phone in the backpack, and set it on the floor.

"Welcome ladies, my name is Miss Monica; I will be your dance instructor. I want you all to have your permission slips signed tonight. Now, please line up in three rows and we will begin."

Everyone in the class scurried into three rows.

"We will start out every class by stretching to warm up our muscles," Miss Monica continued, "and then we will work on body mechanics. Spread your legs to shoulder's width apart and lean forward and touch the floor."

Kim looked at Miss Monica's tall slender frame, well-toned legs, ageless perfect smooth Milky Way complexion, and her hair that was pulled back into a neat bun. She was beautiful, Kim thought; she wished she could look like her. If dancing gave you a body like that, then Kim wanted to dance every day.

The students silently complied with Miss Monica's instructions. Kim stretched her muscles, relaxing into the movements with each new position. After they finished stretching, Miss Monica moved into proper body mechanics, along with hand and leg positioning. Soft music played in the background. As she looked around the room, Kim noticed everyone was focused on the teacher.

"Ladies, I want to teach you two routines. The first song will be a new hip-hop song from your era and the next will be an oldie but goodie from mine," Miss Monica announced. She turned on the stereo. "Teach me how to Dougie" blasted out through the speakers, and everyone started doing the Dougie dance.

Miss Monica chuckled. "Calm down ladies. Let's begin our routine."

It took four attempts to get through the three eight-counts of the dance. Miss Monica continued with the routine, moving her body like a pretzel. Kim felt relieved that the entire class struggled through the dance routine, as she tangled her feet while attempting a spin. No one seemed to notice her missteps, and each time they restarted, the dance became a little more familiar.

The energy Miss Monica gave out was unbelievable. The class was half of her age, but you could see sweat dripping and hear them panting like a bunch of wild animals on the hunt. The sweat trickling down Miss Monica's forehead was the only sign that she was working hard. Kim wiped her eyes and fell in step. The girls practiced for an hour and thirty minutes before they stopped and stretched again.

"See you ladies on Wednesday, and bring your permission slips!" Miss Monica called out to them.

Kim walked over to the wall to grab her bag. She wiped her head and neck with a towel and gulped down her water, trying to put out the fire in her throat.

Most of the girls seemed to be congregating in groups of two to three around the peripheral area of the small room. Looking down, Kim headed for the door and got there at the same time as a sandy brown-haired girl who had wavy curls all over head.

"Hey, what's your name?" the girl asked.

"Kim. What's yours?"

"I'm Marissa and this is my sis, Quaneisha. I haven't seen you around here before. Where are you from?"

Kim wondered why the girl was talking to her.

"I just moved here from Texas," Kim answered. She tried not to sound skeptical. "Did you say sisters?"

"Yep, sisters," Marissa answered.

Their complexions were as different as cream and coffee. Marissa seemed to be the talker of the duo. She was short, petite, and crème colored. Quaneisha was chocolate-brown, around 5'6", with tiny braids covering her head. They both were cute, but they sure didn't look related.

Marissa could see the confusion on Kim's face. "I know we don't look alike, but we have been raised together for the last four years, so I call her my sister."

Kim nodded her head a few times. "Gotcha. I'm adopted too. I get it. I actually just moved in with my new family."

"That's cool," Quaneisha responded. "Want to have lunch with us? They serve free lunches here."

"Sure," Kim answered. She followed the sisters outside and around the building to the lunch line, where each person was handed a white paper boat with a sandwich, apple, potato chips, and milk. The girls walked to a picnic table and sat down to eat.

"What grade are you two in?"

"Tenth," Marissa responded.

Kim beamed. "Me too!"

"How far away do you guys live?" she asked.

"We live at the top of Noeline Ave with our foster mom. I have been in this home since I was a baby and Q since fifth grade," Marissa answered. "My real mom is a loser. She left me when I was a baby, and she hasn't looked back."

"My mom is sick," Quaneisha chimed in, the pain behind her words flashed across her face. "And she lost custody of me when I was ten. I have only been in one home, Miss Ella's, where I met Marissa."

"Girl, you know your mama was hooked on that crack," Marissa said, "and now she serving a three strikes sentence up in Chowchilla."

"My mom is clean now and she has six more years, thank you very much. She has changed. Everyone makes mistakes. If my dad had stayed around, we would have been okay," Quaneisha replied.

Kim could see that Q felt defensive about her mother. And Kim understood. What if she told these girls about her own father? That he used all his money for liquor and couldn't pay the bills, so they had no running water. That he had left her alone when he spent nights in bed with women who were not Maggie. That he had brought drunks into the house and one had tried to rape her.

Kim decided only to reveal some of that. "We cannot control our parents and their mistakes," she began. "My dad became an alcoholic after my mother died, and he didn't care about anybody except himself. He wouldn't change for me. I just hope he changes one day for himself."

"I hope my father does too," Quaneisha replied.

"Forget them, they don't deserve our time

and energy," Marissa chimed in.

The girls finished their lunch, the bread hard to swallow after their conversation. Kim wanted to change the subject. "Where do you guys go to school?" she asked.

"We go to Morse High," Marissa replied. "Will you be attending school out here next year?"

"I hope so, if things work out," Kim answered, thinking of her roommate. "On that note, I better get home."

"We'll walk with you," Quaneisha said.

The girls started walking through the parking lot, heading back toward the hill leading home. Marissa and Quaneisha reached their house first.

"See you Wednesday," they said in unison.

"Okay, bye," Kim said with a wave, and then she walked down the hill.

The conversation opened the pain Kim had been avoiding. She missed her father, even with all his faults. Quaneisha felt the same way. The pain was audible in her voice as she spoke about her mother. Marissa seemed angrier at her mother, but Kim knew she had to be hurt, too.

Kim took out her phone and hurried to dial Tim's telephone number before she could talk herself out of calling. The phone rang, once, twice, three times, and just as she took the phone away from her ear to hang up, she heard, "Hello, hello."

"Hey, Tim. It's Kim. How are you?"

"Hey! I am good, and you sound great," Tim replied.

"I miss you," Kim said, as all the memories from the past flooding back.

Tim had been a true friend. He fed her when she needed food and gave her rides to school when she missed the bus and listened when she had no one else. She missed him deeply. His voice brought back warm feelings about the people in Texas who had truly cared about her.

"How are Kevin and his folks?" Tim asked.

"He is happy and his folks are good people," she answered.

"Are you happy?" he asked.

She sighed. "I'm good. I started a dance class, met some girls, and got a new cell phone. I never imagined life could be this good."

"But?"

"Kevin's sister hates me, and I don't know what to do to fix things. Kevin thinks it will just take time, and I hope he is right."

"Give it some time, it is an adjustment for everybody. Listen to your brother," Tim said. He sounded confident.

Kim hoped that Kevin and Tim were right. If they weren't, she was in for trouble. But she kept those thoughts to herself. Instead, she replied, "Thanks, Tim. Hey, have you seen Keith?"

"He left for college already. Something about an early orientation. But I'll give him your number the next time I see him."

"How about my Dad. Have you seen him?"

"Yeah, he is back next door. You want to talk to him?"

Kim closed her eyes briefly, "Yes."

"Alright. Hold on right quick."

The silent wait was deafening. She wondered what to say to her father. Should she tell him everything so far was good, or would that make him feel bad or even angry? And how did she feel about him? Did she still feel mad that he lied to her about Kevin? He had known all along where Kevin was, but he insisted that he didn't. Should she forgive him? She worried about her brother so much, and spent   hours   with   Keith   prowling   all   the neighborhoods, looking for Kevin after he disappeared. All that time he had been safe and sound, with his own family in California.

"Hello?" Francis said, interrupting Kim's thoughts.

"Hello, Dad."

"How are you?" Francis asked.

"I am good and Kevin is doing well too," Kim added.

"That's good, honey."

Did he really think it was good? Or was he just saying that? His voice didn't sound all that convincing.

"Are you still there, Kim?" her father asked.

"Yes, Dad, I'm still here. How are you feeling?"

"I am doing well, doing my physical therapy and getting stronger," he responded.

"That's good." She let out the breath she was holding in.

She wanted him well, but now she wondered if he had started drinking again.

"Well, I am glad you are okay, honey. I have to get back over to the house and rest. Call me when you can."

"Okay, I love you. Bye, Dad," Kim said.

"I love you too. Bye, honey."

Kim had thought her father would be angry at her for leaving, but he sounded upbeat. Was he faking it? Had he been brief on the phone so he could get back to his alcohol? He didn't ask what she had been doing. It was like he didn't care that she was away. Her feelings were hurt; once again something else was more important than her, but she didn't want to let the phone call ruin her day, which had been one of the best days in a long time.

Dancing felt invigorating, and meeting friends

who were in similar situations helped her feel normal. Life was not perfect for all kids. Talking to Tim and her father had been the icing on the cake. The whole thing had been a little awkward, but it felt good to hear their voices.

Kim headed up the driveway with a little skip in her step. She decided to try to have a talk with Andrea tonight. Tell her she understood that it was hard to have to share her room, but that she wanted to figure out how they could get along. Kim smiled to herself. For the first time she felt optimistic that things might work out.

Chapter 4

Kim walked into the garage carrying her laundry. Today would be a perfect time to get her clothes clean and talk to Andrea. They both were stuck at home together, everyone else was at work or summer school. Maybe she could close the gap that developed between them. It had only been a few weeks, but living in a room with someone was hard when the person ignored you. Kim tried to strike up conversations about dance and school, but Andrea either ignored her or gave short answers. Kevin said Amanda would warm up to her, so Kim remained hopeful. She really wanted to share her experiences with someone. There were so many things she and Andrea could share, such as music, dance, or cute guys. She just had to get Andrea to listen.

Kim placed her sweaty workout clothes into

the washer and watched the clothes twirl around in a circle. Twenty-two minutes left in the cycle; plenty of time to approach Andrea and hash out their differences. Whatever she had done to get off on the wrong foot, she would apologize and everything would be perfect. Someday maybe Andrea would talk to her like she did her friends on the phone.

When Kim entered the family room, she found Andrea curled up on the sofa with the remote in her hand. "Andrea, I wanted to talk to you about something."

Andrea glanced up, acknowledging Kim's presence but saying nothing.

"I feel like we got off on the wrong foot. If I've done anything to upset you, I am sorry," Kim said.

Andrea rolled her eyes.

"Can we fix this?" Kim asked.

"There is nothing to fix. I don't like you. I have to accept you in my room, but I don't have to like it," Andrea replied.

"Why don't you like me?" Kim asked.

"You have no right to be here. Kevin is my biological brother, but you are not even related to us, and you expect my parents to take care of you. Why should you get a free ride?"

Ashamed and humiliated, Kim wanted to cry. The last thing she wanted was to be a burden on anyone and she couldn't let Andrea know her words were cutting deep. Turning her head slightly to blink back the tears, she blew out a long breath. "I have never asked for a free ride. I am willing to work to pay my way. Your parents offered me a home. I have never asked for anything from them, but I'm very grateful to them. What did I do to you?"

"You moved in and took over my room. My parents promised me a larger bed this year and

31

instead of a queen-sized bed, I got another twin-sized bed and you."

"I have no control over any of that stuff. I just want to be friends," Kim replied.

"I don't need any more friends. I will be tolerant because my parents say I have to be, but that is it."

Kim's eyes burned from the unshed tears. "Whatever," Kim said, as she left the room.

Andrea picked up her phone and called one of her friends. Kim overheard her laughing on the phone. "You should have heard her pleading to be my friend. Like I wanted to be friends with a country girl from Texas. Really, I don't even know why she is here, my parents are crazy to start taking in strays. Come pick me up. A trip to the mall will cheer me up. I'll get dressed and see you in fifteen minutes."

Kim squeezed her fists and walked back out to the garage. That little twisted spoiled brat was the most selfish person Kim had ever met. She would rather have Kim live on the street than share a bedroom with her. There was nothing Kim could do to fix this riff. She had never met anyone so unwilling to compromise.

Kim vowed to stay out of Andrea's way, but she wouldn't apologize anymore for being in the house. She had to fit in so that Allison and Robert wouldn't send her away.

Kim placed her clothes in the dryer and walked out of the garage. She headed through the front door just as Andrea's friend walked up.

Everything on the girl looked fake: from her makeup to her blue eyes to the wig she wore. Somewhere underneath all that flashy designer wear was a decent looking girl.

"Oh hi, I'm Shea, Andrea's friend."

"Hi, I'm Kim. Come on in. I'll get Andrea."

Kim let Andrea know her friend was there.

"Hey, girl," Andrea said, as she walked toward the door, "let's go."

Shea looked over at Kim one last time and walked out the door behind Andrea.

"Nice meeting you too," Kim whispered to the closing door.

Feeling like a good run would clear her head, Kim headed to the bedroom to get dressed. Just then her cell phone started ringing. She smiled—it was Tim's number. She needed to hear an old friend's voice right now. He had perfect timing. He always seemed to know when she needed a shoulder to lean on.

"Hey honey, I decided to call you back," Francis announced on the other end.

Kim was not in the mood for Francis, but she sat down on her bed anyway. "Oh hi, Dad, I thought you were Tim. How are you?"

"I'm fine. I got a new job at the chicken plant. It will start in a couple of weeks, so it gives me time to work a little more with my physical therapist. Those boys may have shot me, but I am strong and my body is healing nicely. What are you doing?"

"I am enjoying the summer. I started a dance class and it's fun."

"How are they treating you out there?"

"Everyone has been real nice," she lied, hoping he didn't notice the hesitation in her voice.

"No one will treat you like family, that's for sure. Listen, I've been thinking, and I want you to come home. You have seen your brother and had a nice little visit. Now it is time to come back home."

"I just got here. This is not what we discussed before I left," Kim said. Her father had told her it was her decision, and now he was changing his mind. "As I remember you only had time for your bottle. I am not coming back to your drinking and reckless behavior, Dad."

"I have changed. I am sorry about the drinking, but we are family and you need to come home."

"I am enrolled in this summer dance class, and I am finally having fun like kids are supposed to do. I don't want to leave now. Plus, you said it was up to me to make the decision. Are you going back on your word?"

"I am the parent and I made a mistake letting you make the decision. Now as a parent, it is my job to decide where you live. I say that is in Texas with me."

How dare her father be so selfish? He had taken her through hell, and now he had a forgive-and-forget attitude about it. Kim wanted to scream.

"You haven't been able to take care of me. Living without food, water, and electricity is not how a kid is supposed to live. I have never asked for much from you, but a parent is supposed to provide the basics. Do you have the water turned back on or the phone?"

"The water is back on, but I don't need a phone. I am getting my life back together. I will allow you to finish the summer, but when school starts, I want you home. This will give me a little more time to get things straight here."

Kim sighed. "We can talk more about this later, okay? I have to go now."

"Okay, we can talk later, but my decision is final. Oh wait, Tim wants to speak to you."

"Hey, Kim, just a minute," Tim said. "Bye, Mr. Celestine! You're welcome."

Kim could hear Tim close the door, then pick the phone back up.

"You okay?" he asked.

"I am shocked. I just got here and he wants me to come back. I don't get it. Was he drunk?"

"No, he seemed sober. Look you gotta do what is best for you. Do you like it there?"

"I like it. I'm still not getting along with Kevin's sister, but I have everything I need. And I started this dance class that's cool. I'm trying to be a part of the family."

"I know what you mean."

"Enough about me, Tim. What's going on with my Dad? Does he have the water and lights on next door?"

"It still looks pretty dark over there to me, but he has not been borrowing water from us. He hasn't been home much, so I don't know where he has been staying."

"Well, I am going to talk to Kevin and see what he thinks. Life is not perfect anywhere, so I will weigh my options and make a decision. At least I have the summer to decide."

"He may change his mind when he thinks about it more. I am sure he wants you to be happy," Tim said. "Hey, I have to go. I have football practice. Call me any time, though, okay? I am always here for you."

"I know, Tim. Thanks for everything."

"No problem. Talk to you later."

"Yep, talk to you later."

Kim ended the call and sat there for a moment. Now more than ever, she really needed some fresh air. So, she changed quickly, threw on her running shoes, grabbed her key to the house, and headed out the door.

Her father and Andrea seemed to be on the same team. Both wanted Kim out of California. What about what she wanted and her dreams? She finally felt like her dreams of college were attainable, and now her father had dropped this bomb on her. She still loved him, despite all his mistakes, and wanted to remain a part of his life, but he had proved himself incapable of taking care of her. She thought it would be easier for him alone, and now he wanted her back.

Kim ran on, allowing her thoughts to flood through her mind. She had failed miserably at mending the fences with Andrea. How would she live in the same room with someone who thought she was the enemy? Maybe going back to her dad would be better. What if coming close to death had changed him. She never waited around to see if he had stopped drinking for good. Did she owe him a chance to rebuild their family? Her mother, Maggie, had wanted the family to stay together. Kevin left first and then Kim, and now she and Kevin were together again.

Sweat ran down her forehead as she continued running. She made a turn on Noeline Avenue, then headed back up toward the house. Kevin would be off work soon and she would talk to him. Maybe a miracle might happen and Andrea would open her heart and let Kim in.

Chapter 5

Kim shivered as she spooned another bite of her sweet cream flavored ice cream, with caramel and pecans, into her mouth. "Heaven," she said, rolling her eyes. "I needed this."

"I love this place. My parents brought us here after church when I first got here. It always makes me feel comforted," Kevin replied, as he bit into his waffle cone. "Next time you got to get the waffle cone."

She laughed. "You are getting crumbs everywhere."

They both laughed as he picked up the crumbs and added it to his ice cream. "Waffle sprinkles, good stuff," Kevin commented, and licked the ice cream.

This day was getting better. She had missed the good times with her brother, and now they could resume their close relationship. It had been lonely, quiet, and sad at the house with Kevin away. Now she could make up for lost time. This family made her brother happy, his body was relaxed, and he was joking around. He was different from his old self. A tentative smile crossed Kim's face as she thought about it. Change appeared to be a good thing for him, though.

Just then her cell phone started ringing.

"Hey honey," Francis announced on the other end.

"Oh hi, Dad. How are you?" Kim asked as she looked out the window of the car. It felt awkward talking to her father right then. The atmosphere in the car just changed from warm to cold, and even though she didn't dare look at her brother, the chill was coming from him. Fixing the broken ties between her father and brother would take time. Kim hoped she could be the catalyst for that.

"I got a new job at the chicken plant. It will start in a couple of weeks, so it gives me time to work a little more with my physical therapist. Those boys may have shot me but I am strong and my body is healing nicely. Enough about me I called to see how you are doing?"

"I am enjoying the summer. I started a dance class and it's fun," she replied.

"How are they treating you out there?" her father asked.

"Everyone has really nice," she lied, hoping he didn't notice the hesitation in her voice. She couldn't bear to tell him about Andrea.

"No one will treat you like family, that's for sure. I have been thinking and I want you to come home. You have seen your brother and had a nice little visit, now it is time to come back home."

"I just got here," Kim answered, taken by

surprise. Her father had told her it was her decision, and now he was changing his mind. What was this all about? Kim's heart skipped a beat, how could she go back, right now? "I am not ready to come back."

"Damn straight you are not," Kevin spat. Kim held up one finger to get her brother to halt his comments.

"I have changed. I am sorry about the drinking, but we are family and you need to come home."

"I am enrolled in this summer dance class, and I am finally having fun like kids are supposed to do. I don't want to leave now. Plus, you said it was up to me to make the decision; now you are going back on your word," Kim replied.

"That's what he does best—lie," Kevin mumbled. "I bet he is saying that he is through drinking, when he was drunk last night."

Kim tried to ignore her brother's statements. Listening to her father was hard enough. Now they were antagonizing her from two different directions. Their father had lied a few times, but he was the adult, and he wouldn't lie to her again, would he?

"I am the parent," Francis said firmly, "and I made a mistake letting you make the decision. Now as a parent, it is my job to decide where you live. I say that is in Texas with me."

It had been a long time since he acted like a parent, and now he threw that statement out there. Kim thought back to her father's idea of taking care of her. He didn't have a clue.

Kim proceeded cautiously. "Do you have the water turned back on or the phone?"

"The water is back on, but I don't need a phone. I am getting my life back together, slowly but surely. I will allow you to finish the summer out there, but when school starts, I want you home. This will give me a little more time to get things straight here."

"We can talk more about this later," Kim replied. "I have to go now."

"Okay, we can talk later, but my decision is final."

Kim exhaled and ended the call.

"So?" Kevin asked, not looking up.

"I am shocked. I just got here and he already wants me to come back. I don't get it."

"He's a drunk. I hope you aren't falling for that BS," Kevin spat.

Kim felt torn because she loved both her father and her brother. She didn't know what to say. "You know no one is perfect."

Kevin shook his head. "How soon you forget. Remember sitting outside in the 110-degree Texas heat while he gambled and drank. He didn't care then, and he doesn't care now."

"No, I remember. And I remember waking up to find my brother missing. We lost our Mom and I lost you, but you expected me to get past what you did. Why can't you get past what he did?" Kim shot back at her brother. "He deserves more from you as his son. Like I said, everyone makes mistakes."

Kevin slumped his shoulders over, eased off the accelerator, and eased his grip on the steering wheel. He turned to Kim and said, "Those are two different things. You can't compare the two. It's like apples and oranges."

"Explain please, because apples and oranges are both fruit."

Both Kevin and Francis had hurt Kim, but Kevin didn't seem to remember. He didn't remember how she worried and searched for him while all along he was safe and sound in San Diego. She even filed a missing person report with the police. Sure, their father had done many things that weren't right, but

Kim couldn't find it in her heart to hate him. How could Kevin?

"Kim, I know you don't understand."

"You're right. I don't understand. And you never tried to explain it to me."

"Don't you understand? The only reason I stayed for as long as I did was because of you. When he stole the money I worked hard for, that was the last straw for me. I lost all respect for him then. A man doesn't steal from his kids. Mom left an inheritance for us to go to college, not to bail out an incompetent parent."

Kevin pulled the car in front of the house and turned off the engine. "The only thing I am sorry about is that I left you. I didn't mean to hurt you. I just couldn't stay with him another second."

"You couldn't leave me a note or call, so I wouldn't worry? I cried myself to sleep because I thought I lost you too," Kim replied. "I am not saying what Dad did was right, but alcoholism is a disease and you don't hate sick people. He needs help, not attitude or constant reminders of what he's done wrong."

"My real dad here in San Diego has shown me what a real man looks like. So no, I can't condone or forget Francis's actions. It is a constant thorn in my side, and I can't forgive him. I am so sorry I left you in that hell, but you have a soft spot for the man and I didn't see you leaving him to come with me. I promise you; I was going to come back for you. Please forgive me."

"I have forgiven you. All I'm saying is, it was hard without you, and not knowing what happened to you, the worst. I was able to see how much you shielded me from the drinking and reckless behavior, but I also believe he is a good man without alcohol. Before mom died, he was great. Her death was devastating to him also."

"He should have gotten it together for us, but he didn't care enough to try," Kevin whispered.

"I want him to get better. I would never stop loving you and I can't stop loving him," Kim said.

"Kim, it's just not that simple. When I think of him, I get so angry. You have always been blinded by him, but I see the real him and I hate him."

"I hope one day you can find it in your heart to forgive him the same way I forgave him," Kim replied as she got out of the car and walked toward the house.

Chapter 6

Kim turned over, pulled the purple blanket over her head, and blocked out the morning sun. She tossed and turned all night, trying to make sense of her brother's negative attitude toward their father, and now she felt exhausted, mentally, and physically. She needed one of them to give in. The sad truth was that neither one looked ready to budge.

Finally giving up on sleep, she opened her eyes, pulled the cover down and glanced at her flashing phone. There was one missed text message from Kevin and one missed alert from her calendar flashing, "Dance in 15 minutes!"

Kim dropped the phone on the nightstand and raced around the room, dressing quickly in grey sweats. Then she ran out of the house.

She started out walking at a quick pace, then picked up the speed to a brisk jog. She thought about Kevin and his stubborn attitude. She would try again with him later. They had not been raised to be so heartless. She figured it must have been a family trait; look at Andrea and her selfish attitude.

Things had not improved in that area. Having lost her own mother, Kim couldn't help the jealousy she felt when Andrea interacted with Allison.

Kim missed Maggie terribly. Even though Maggie had not been her biological mother, she loved Kim unconditionally. It was still hard to hold back tears when she thought about it. A tear slipped down her cheek, as she ran across the street toward the park. How come her life couldn't get better and stay that way? Why did bad things have to happen to good people, Kim wondered? She couldn't help feeling a sorry for herself.

Kim continued running through the park until she reached the rec room where dance class was being held. The class was starting to do their warmups, so she quickly dropped her bag and joined in. As she stretched, bending at the waist, touching the floor, then separating her legs, one in front, one behind, her thoughts wandered back to the previous night's events and the major decision that she had to make: follow her dad's wishes or disobey him and stay in California. Kevin was too upset for her to talk to, but she needed someone to listen. She decided she would ask Tim what he thought about her father's demand. He could help her sort through the facts and reach a conclusion. She wouldn't have to make the decision alone. He would remember what life had been like for her in Texas before and after Maggie's death.

The dance class started to work on the routines that they learned the previous session. They were learning a jazz-square and a chasse' move. Soon

Kim began concentrating on her dancing. The jazz square was easy; you just stepped forward with your right foot, then crossed over with the left foot, then stepped back with the right. The chasse' move was like skipping, but everyone kept getting tangled up on the steps. You had to step forward with your right foot and bring your left foot up behind you and then step off with your right. It was fast and hard to learn at first, but Kim starting to get the hang of it. Forward with your right, left up behind, then steps off with your right. Continuing the routine until she was drenched with sweat two hours later, Kim grabbed her bag and headed toward her new friends. "Where are you guys off to?" she asked, wiping her forehead.

"We are walking to the taco shop. Do you want to go with us?" Marissa asked.

"I didn't bring any money with me." Kim looked over at Quaneisha, who was silent through the whole exchange; did Marissa always speak for both of them? "Can we walk by my house so I can grab some?"

Quaneisha was the tall Amazon, with a sleek muscular figure. She rarely spoke, but her eyes held depth and emotion. Marissa was the hot tamale – loud, direct, all bark with little bite, and barely five feet tall.

"You can pay us back next time. We have enough for three orders of rolled tacos," Marissa answered.

"Thanks," Kim replied.

"Quaneisha and I fed the neighbor's dog while they were out of town, so we have some extra cash. Let's drop off our stuff at the house and then we will walk up the hill to the taco shop," Marissa said.

"Marissa, we should just take our stuff with

us," Quaneisha replied.

"It will be cool. She had a doctor's appointment this morning," Marissa said.

Quaneisha sighed and continued walking. Kim watched the exchange between the two, wondering why Quaneisha wanted to avoid going home. Was their home a mess like hers had become in Texas? Did their foster mom drink like Francis? Maybe they had no electricity.

Quaneisha bit her lip and folded her arms, visibly agitated. Marissa, however, was calm and relaxed. They walked out of the park, headed down the street toward Noeline Avenue, and started talking about the class.

"Marissa, you were able to do the dance after the first time she showed it to us. That was awesome," Kim said.

"I love dancing. I want to dance in the ballet or be the next video vixen," Marissa answered, as she went from a pirouette to a body roll.

"I could see that," Kim responded, in awe of her friend's quick fluid movements. She could definitely have a career in dance. "Can you teach me that turn?"

"Sure, we can practice at the park. You'll get the step, don't worry," Marissa answered. "Q and I practice at home every day. She is a great dancer, too."

"I do it for fun and exercise," Quaneisha responded. "I could use the practice too. You are the dancer in the family, Marissa. If you were older, you could get a job now."

Marissa looked up and tensed. "When I do get a job, we are getting our own place."

"That's great. I want to be a doctor when I get older," Kim revealed.

"For real? I want to be a pediatric nurse,"

46

Quaneisha responded.

Quaneisha and Marissa's house was only a few blocks from the park. As they approached the house, Kim saw that a red minivan occupied the driveway. Quaneisha gripped herself tighter and continued biting her bottom lip.

"She's home," Quaneisha said, slowing down.

"I know. I saw the car. I'll go inside since I have to get my wallet. Give me your bag and I'll put it away."

"Okay," Quaneisha answered.

Marissa was walking up the driveway, headed toward the front door, when she saw her foster mom heading in her direction.

"Bitch, what are you doing here?" her foster mom asked.

"I forgot something, and we needed to drop our bags off," Marissa answered, boldly.

"Hurry up and get your ass back outside. Quaneisha, who is that? I hope you don't think this is the local handout. It ain't happening up in here!" her foster mother barked.

"This is our friend, Kim, from the dance class. We are just waiting on Marissa," Quaneisha answered evenly.

"Hello," Kim said.

Miss Ella was an overpowering 5'11" robust woman, chocolate brown, with a curly wig. She looked manly, with her shaved chin. She wore pink leggings with a white oversized top, and a pair of white tennis shoes, her clothes barely containing her large frame. Kim waited for the greeting that never came.

Miss Ella looked Kim up and down. "Well, you heard me. No extra kids in my damn house."

"Yes, ma'am," Quaneisha replied.

Marissa ran back outside, with a small

backpack over her shoulders. "We will see you later, Miss Ella."

"Be here before dark. I'm headed to the doctor. My house better be like I left it or I'm gonna beat somebody's ass," Miss Ella replied, slamming her car door.

The three girls silently walked back up the sidewalk away from the house. Kim was shocked by what she witnessed. Her friends' foster mother seemed like an evil demon. How could anyone live with someone like that? It must be awful to live somewhere and not be able to call it home. Kim knew how it felt to be insecure in your own house. Her life experience wasn't that much different from the girls.

"My life in Texas was really bad," Kim offered. "My dad would leave me home alone while he hung out with his girlfriend and drank with his friends," Kim told her new friends. "That is why I left Texas. He couldn't pay the bills or buy food for us. I hated my life there."

Quaneisha looked up. "I hate our life here. At least my parents loved me. But not her. We are just there so she can get a check."

"I can't stand her," Marissa said. "My mom is out on the streets hooking to cover her drug habit. I think life with her is better than staying in that house."

"My mom wants us to be a family again when she gets out of jail. She made a few mistakes," Quaneisha said. "She wrote a hot check to cover a car she wanted to buy. Everyone got all bent out of shape about it, even though she gave the car back. I mean, they should have let her go. After all, they got their stuff back."

Kim was sure the legal system didn't work like that. If you commit a crime, you did the time. That was the law. She knew sometimes the legal system didn't work, like when her father convinced the judge to hand over her mother's insurance money, which quickly disappeared. But she didn't correct her new friend. Instead, she simply said, "That's messed up." She wanted Quaneisha to know that she supported her.

"We got each other, Quaneisha," Marissa replied.

"I know, but life is messed up," Quaneisha said.

"You got that right," Kim agreed.

The girls walked in the taco shop and ordered three sets of rolled tacos with guacamole.

"Have you ever had Mexican food?" Marissa asked.

"No," Kim replied.

"You will love it. I could eat this every day."

"We have to hide the money we make or she will want a cut of it. I don't mind contributing to the household, but when she treats us like dogs, I don't want to give her nothing," Quaneisha said. "I asked her to help me buy a pair of twenty-dollar shoes, to replace a pair of worn out ones, and she told me I could go barefoot."

"She had just got her nails done, and she just cashed the check she gets for us," Marissa added.

"I found a pair on clearance at Ross, trying to save her some money. Now we work odd jobs and keep the money to ourselves," Quaneisha said.

"Do you have anyone you could talk to about her?" Kim asked.

"Our social worker is just glad she got us placed with someone. No one wants teens. They think we are just trouble," Marissa said.

"Once, we did mention something to the social worker, and Miss Ella made us go to bed without dinner for a week," Quaneisha added.

"We keep each other going and keep our mouths shut," Quaneisha replied. "When we turn 18, we will get our own place together. You can come too, if you want."

"If you stay close enough to San Diego State University, then count me in, because I am going to college. I promised my mother I would. She died two years ago, and I have to keep my promise," Kim replied.

Marissa and Quaneisha nodded their heads.

Kim continued. "I am staying with my brother's biological parents. See, after our mother died, we both found out we were adopted. He ran away and found his real parents because our adopted father is a drunk. They were kind enough to let me stay too."

"You are so lucky," Marissa said.

"I thought so too, until my dad called from Texas and said I had to go back at the end of summer. I don't know what to do. He says things are better, but he lies so well that I can't believe him. Things were so bad before. I'm afraid to go back."

"You don't have to decide today, but we want you to stay. We are here for you, and we will help you figure out something before the end of summer," Marissa said.

It felt good to have people on her side, Kim thought. Marissa and Quaneisha were turning out to be good friends, kind of like Tim at home.

"Most kids treat us like we have the plague because we are in foster care, but you have been real," Quaneisha replied. "I'll grab our tacos."

Kim tasted the crunchy rolled taco covered with guacamole and cheese. She smiled. "These are delicious. I have a new favorite food. You're right, I could eat this every day."

The three girls laughed and finished their

lunch. As they walked out of the taco shop, four guys walked in wearing Morse High football practice jerseys. Kim turned her head to follow the guys.

"Great place to have lunch," Kim said.

"Great scenery too," Marissa added. "But that is better," she whistled, pointing at a passing car filled with bandana-wearing guys, arms hanging out of the window, throwing hand signs up like the hearing impaired.

"Those are thugs," Quaneisha commented.

"Just because they are Hispanic doesn't make them thugs," Marissa argued.

"But the gang signs they threw up to the football players seals the deal for me—gang bangers," Quaneisha said."

"Don't judge a book by its cover. That's your favorite saying. We don't know that they are bad, and they are definitely fine, like that rapper Drake," Marissa said smoothly and with a grin. "Something about a guy who wears his clothes baggy and has a cool confidence in his walk and the way he talks is so attractive to me."

"Play with fire and you will get burned, my grandmother always said. You can't compare a working artist to a street thug. Sometimes I don't know where your head is," Quaneisha said, rolling her eyes.

Kim was shocked into silence by the display. Her earlier feelings about Quaneisha were correct. She was very wise and passionate. But Marissa, she seemed to like trouble.

The girls started walking back toward Miss Ella's house. Just as they were about to cross the street, a red car sped by, barely missing them.

"You guys are pathetic!" Andrea yelled from the car.

"Who is that slut?" Marissa asked.

"My brother's biological sister, whom I share a room with. Did I mention she can't stand me?" Kim responded. "She is making my time here awful. Sorry you had to witness her acting stupid."

"Don't worry about her, because we aren't," Quaneisha replied.

"I can beat her ass for you," Marissa said, puffing her chest up and standing on her toes.

Kim laughed at how quickly her friends rallied to her side, "Naw, that's not necessary. I'll handle it."

Kim walked her friend's home, then headed for her house. Andrea tried to embarrass her in front of her friends and they had been able to ignore her stupid behavior. The constant conflict between her and Andrea was exhausting. Kim tried to compromise with her, without success. She would not, be insulted by that selfish brat. If Andrea wanted to act up, Kim decided she would not let her walk all over her feelings. Andrea did not have to like her, but Kim felt that she deserved to be treated with respect. Kim would let Andrea know how she felt, or Allison would know how Andrea was acting.

As she walked home, Kim thought about her life. Kim was in a foster home too, an outsider taken in by a family; afraid to upset the balance, walking on eggshells. She had two new friends and hanging out with them had been great. But more important, she realized that she identified with them. Everyone had problems, some big and some small. No family was perfect, and it felt good to share her past with someone. Since she'd come to live with Allison and Robert, no one asked her about Texas and how she had survived. It was like the elephant in the middle of the room, everyone avoiding the subject. Talking about the elephant sure felt better than walking around it. Tomorrow she would call Tim.

Chapter 7

Kim stood in front of the mirror in her bedroom brushing her hair. She brushed and brushed, releasing the tension she felt. Acclimating to a new environment was hard enough and then added to it the tension of whether she would stay or go back to Texas, and Kim felt lost. The only lifeline she had in California was Kevin and his bitterness toward their father made him biased. Surely Tim, who was like brother to her, could offer some solutions to her dilemma.

The smell of breakfast drew her attention away from her thoughts.

It was nice having food in the house and parents preparing meals again. It was a fairytale come true.

On the way to the kitchen, she walked pass

her brother's room, looking in she saw him lacing up his Nike tennis shoes. Their eyes met and he exhaled, "Kim, hang on a second."

She leaned on the doorframe, "I don't want us to fight. Let's agree to disagree right now. I have some strong feelings about Francis, and you have always looked for the good in him. He doesn't deserve you. However, I can respect your feelings, but do me a favor and gather the facts. Respect my feelings, even if you don't agree with them. Love you, sis," he said. Then he kissed her temple and headed to work.

Kim watched him leave and turned back to her room, forgetting breakfast. Instead, she grabbed her phone to gather some facts. She sat down on the bed and scrolled through her short phone list. She originally thought about Tim, but now it seemed her friend Keith would be the best source of information. He was the friend who kept her grounded when the world around her fell apart. He also volunteered on the local police force, so if her father was telling the truth, Keith would be able to validate it. He could give her the facts she needed.

Her heart skipped a beat as she dialed him, remembering how cute and sexy Keith was at a muscled six feet one frame. The phone started ringing, and Kim held her breath.

"Hello?" Keith answered. "I'm not buying nothing."

Kim laughed. "Not even dinner for a friend," she teased.

"Kim! You have made my day. I was just thinking about you. I am so glad to hear from you."

His voice was always so strong and comforting. He was the good part of home that she missed. Keith came into her life when she felt humiliated by a boy from school and abandoned by her brother, by listening and making sure she remained safe. Kim leaned back on her bed, picturing his concerned face smiling at her.

"Tell me everything. Is everything working out?" he asked.

"I am fine. I just...I don't know where to start. I feel like I live with the Cosby's. Except for Kevin's wicked sister, everything is great. I am taking dance and I've met some new friends. It's cool."

"But?" Kevin responded.

Kim sighed. "Well Kevin's sister really hates me. She says I invaded her space."

"Is she treating you bad?" he asked.

"More like ignoring my existence entirely. Kevin says it will take time to develop a relationship with her. I personally think that will never happen. It makes for an awkward room, but his parents are so nice."

"I agree with Kevin, his sister will probably come around, she has been the only girl for years, so it is a major adjustment for her. Still, no one treats my Kim badly. I'll speak with her if you like."

Kim smiled. "No that won't be necessary, but thanks."

"You sure? I could arrest her," he teased. "How has it been being reunited with Kevin?"

"It feels different, I think we both grew while we were apart and now he has his biological family. It's hard to see where I fit in."

"First of all, you guys grew up together and that's why he pushed to get you to California. If he didn't care, he wouldn't have done that. Second, he's adjusting, just like you are, so you have to give him some slack. Third, no pity parties for you. Enjoy the opportunity you have been given," Keith proclaimed.

He was always so honest, and that's why she enjoyed his company. He scolded her when she made mistakes and praised her when she did well. He was right. She hadn't looked at anyone else's point of view except her own. "Well now that I am enrolled in dance and trying to get into a routine, my father calls and wants me to return to Texas. He says he is off the alcohol and starting a new job, but I don't know what to believe anymore. What do you think?"

"I don't know if he is still drinking, but I saw him walking home last night while I was out on patrol. He needs to get help if he plans to quit drinking. Otherwise, he is setting himself up to fail. I hope he can quit; however, it is unfair to take you from a stable environment to bring you back to a place where you both would be struggling. What parent wants their child to live like that?"

"If you see him out drinking, please text me. If he is lying, I need to know. I am not going back to that drama," Kim responded.

"I will, but I want you to think about yourself this summer. Have some fun. Things have a way of working themselves out."

"Thanks," she said.

"And you know my line is always open if you need to talk," Keith informed her.

Think about herself, now that's a great concept. Maybe her father would forget about her and Kim's problems would be solved. When he drank, he lost focus anyway, just like when he neglected to pay the water bill and forced them to borrow water from their neighbor. Worrying won't solve the problem, and Keith gave her some good information. Kim could continue to gather information and either her father would make a miraculous recovery, or he'd drown himself in his lies and alcohol.

Chapter 8

Kim wanted to have her new friends over, but she was uneasy about asking permission. What if Robert and Allison said no or made her answer a million questions about them? Her friends couldn't have people over to their houses, so maybe she wasn't allowed to invite friends over either. After all, these weren't her biological parents. Andrea made that crystal clear.

Kim sighed to herself.

She heard Allison in the kitchen putting away groceries and she wanted to catch her before the other kids came out to help. Just in case the answer was no, she could sulk back to the bedroom and no one else would know.

Kim walked the hallway, feeling like she was walking the last mile to an execution. Nervous energy bubbled inside her stomach, though she kept reminding herself that this was a simple question and Kevin's parents were reasonable people. It was crazy to get all worked up over this. It would be yes or no, and either way she could handle it. Kim took a deep breath, held her head high and walked into the kitchen.

"Good morning, Allison" Kim said.

"Morning, Kim. Put away the milk and juice for me. I've been meaning to talk to you. How's everything going?" Allison asked.

"Great, I love my dance class and it's been wonderful here," Kim answered, leaving out the part about Andrea's nasty attitude.

"Good! I want you to feel at home, okay? If you need anything just ask."

Perfect opening, Kim smiled as she looked up from the refrigerator. "Well, I've met two friends from dance class. Could they come over? I didn't know if I'm allowed to have friends over, but I was hoping they could stop by for a little while this afternoon. They have been so nice to me."

"Of course, they can come over. I would love to meet them."

Kim released the air from her lungs. "Thank you!"

"Come help me bring in the rest of the groceries," Allison said, as she placed the food in the cabinet.

Kim went out and helped bring in the last few bags, then watched as Allison made breakfast. Two skillets sizzled on the stove, while Allison stirred the eggs and flipped the bacon. The smell of bacon competed with the smell of hot biscuits throughout the house making Kim's stomach growl. "Call the other kids to breakfast, please."

Kim skipped to the hallway, knocked on each

door and announced that breakfast was ready. With the food sitting out on the center of the kitchen table, Allison said a blessing and started passing the dishes around the table. Today is going to be wonderful, Kim thought. Even her sour-looking roommate couldn't make her feel bad.

The table was quiet as everyone ate. Kim smiled as she remembered Maggie cooking meals like this. The smell of the bacon took her back to seeing her mother in her bright yellow kitchen. Those were happy times, and these were happy times. Kim looked around the table at all the satisfied faces. The food tasted like the cook cared.

After breakfast, Kim helped clean the kitchen with the rest of the kids. They worked like a well-oiled machine. Kim placed the stopper in the sink and filled it with hot, soapy water. Then she washed the dishes, while Kevin rinsed and dried and put the dishes away. Julian swept the floor and cleaned the counters while Andrea cleaned the table and put the food away. The kitchen was immaculate in less than twenty minutes. After the work was done, Kim grabbed her cell phone to call her friends.

"Hey Q, you guys want to come over this afternoon?" Kim asked. "We can hang out. The parents say it's cool."

"Yeah, what's the address?" Quaneisha answered.

"Fourth house on the right, on Noeline Lane, 8354," Kim responded.

This was exciting for Kim. Nothing could ruin her day. She glanced over at Andrea painting her lips. She was gorgeous, except for that little thing called attitude, which for Kim shattered the illusion of beauty. Her beautiful light brown eyes and bone straight hair stood out against her caramel colored skin. Girls dreamed about having her perfect looks, then add designer labeled outfits, which Andrea made a point to talk about them to her friends on the phone.

Andrea was leaving with some friends. Kim overheard her say so in a conversation on the phone earlier. The incident from the other day—with Andrea yelling out the window—still burned whenever Kim thought about it. She promised herself that she would let Andrea know that her behavior was not okay. She couldn't keep stuffing it down.

"Andrea, I get it, you don't like me, that's fine. We don't have to hang out or be friends, but don't yell out the car at me like I am some animal," Kim said, releasing the tension she felt.

"You don't give me orders," Andrea responded.

"This is your last warning. Next time I will tell your parents. Just be nice. God, how hard is that?" Kim said as she left the room.

Relief flooded through Kim; she hated bullies and people who took advantage of others. She remembered her fight at school with the bully back in Texas. It was after Maggie died and a girl attacked Kim, forcing her to defend herself. It was hard, but she learned then to stand up for what was right. Andrea could hate Kim all she wanted, but yelling at her and calling her names was off limits.

When her friends rang the doorbell, Kim let them into the house and introduced them to Allison, who gave them a half smile then led them to the back patio so they could hang out privately. Marissa wore a pair of baby-blue sweat Capri pants with a stretched white t-shirt and Quaneisha wore black shorts with a black faded tank top with 'Pink" spelled out in red across her chest. Kim looked at her friends' old clothes, Marissa's frizzy hair and Quaneisha's thick coarse hair. They reminded Kim of the country town she grew up in. Those clothes would be perfect in Omaha, but here, in her new world, they felt out of place. Everything in Allison's house could have come right out of the fashion magazines, color coordinated, neat and clean. Bringing her friends to her house was like that old show "Fresh Prince" where the kid came from the ghetto and moved to the rich neighborhood. What would they think? How would they feel? How well did she know these girls? Suddenly Kim felt a little awkward.

"It was cool of your parents to let us come over and hang out," Marissa said.

"Yeah it was pretty nice," Kim answered. "Have you guys been practicing?"

"No, not really," Marissa answered. "Our foster mom doesn't like us to play our music, and it's kind of hard to practice with earphones on."

"I haven't found time to practice yet either. I don't have my own sound system and I won't ask to borrow my roommate's because she hates me," Kim responded.

"She seems…special," Marissa responded.

"Very," Kim said with a giggle.

"You ladies want some lemonade?" Allison asked, as she stepped out on the patio.

"Yes, thank you," they answered in unison, taking the glasses from the silver tray.

"Here are some cookies, too," Allison said, as she set down the platter of homemade chocolate chip cookies. Allison made everything look like some fancy tea party. This was perfect for Andrea's friends, but a little out of place for Kim's. The shocked look on their faces clearly showed this was odd for them.

"You got it good," Marissa joked.

"She is great," Kim said. "It still feels like a dream compared to my life in Texas. I still feel like I am going to wake up and see the world I lived in before."

"Do you ever miss your real parents?" Quaneisha asked.

"Yeah, I miss my mom who died and my father who raised me, even though he's got some issues," Kim answered. "You miss yours?"

"I miss them every day." Quaneisha answered. "At least they loved me."

"I love you, girl," Marissa added.

"You got me too," Kim answered.

"Thanks, you, guys, but I don't have a home. I was ripped away from my parents to live in a hellhole. So, what if my parents did illegal stuff to get by. They loved me," Quaneisha said softly.

"My mom is on the streets hooked on crack, turning tricks. She didn't give a damn about me or my sisters, only her gang friends. She would rather get high than feed her kids, so I don't miss that life. Our life is crappy now, but I don't want to live with a drug addict either," Marissa replied.

"What about you, Q? What were your parents like?" Kim asked.

"I miss my dad a lot, "Quaneisha said. "He would always wake me up when he came home from a night out working and give me a kiss goodnight. He wrote me a letter and he was talking about how the system is always out to get the black man. He said, he was set up by our neighbor who was jealous of his family. Now they want to give him seven to ten years for possession with intent to sell," Quaneisha explained. "That neighbor tore our family apart."

"Your dad's actions tore your family apart," Marissa countered. "If you do the crime, you have to be willing to do your time. He was a drug dealer. No one lied on him. He got caught."

"We have to pay when we make bad choices

and so do parents. My dad went to jail for drunk driving," Kim shared. "He loved to blame others for his shortcomings. But if I have to live with my mistakes, he does too. It doesn't make me love him less. I just wish his mistakes didn't affect me so much."

"I hear you guys," Quaneisha replied, "but it sucks because he was quitting the business. My mom kept using his product, so he was losing money."

"I know you wish things had happened differently. Me too," Kim responded. "My mom's death started a downward spiral and split our family apart. Many days I wished she was still alive."

"My dad is in Chula Vista county jail awaiting sentencing. He wants me to visit him before they transfer him somewhere far away."

"You going?" Kim asked.

"I want to, but I don't want to go alone, and our foster mom won't let Marissa go with me. She says the social worker would not allow it," Quaneisha answered.

"How are you going?" Kim asked.

"The bus."

"I'll ask to go with you to Chula Vista. I went to the mall out there when I first got here and I will go to the mall while you visit your dad," Kim said. "I'm sure it'll be okay."

"That would be great. I want to go Saturday morning," Quaneisha said, smiling for the first time since she arrived. "Would that work?"

"Sure. Maybe I'll meet you guys for lunch at the taco shop after the visit," Marissa said.

"Sounds good," Quaneisha replied. "We have to go now. We got a babysitting gig. I need to get money for our bus ride."

Kim told her friends goodbye and watched them walk down her cul de sac. Parents could make life hard on kids. She thought her life in Texas was bad, but her friends had a hard life too. Kim felt a little guilty for looking at them like they didn't belong in her new world. She didn't really fit in this new world either. She had tattered clothes in her old suitcase under her bed. Just because she was living in a better neighborhood now didn't give her the right to judge others. In fact, it should help her sympathize with her new friends. Kim sighed and swore she would never raise her kids the way her father and Marissa and Quaneisha's parents raised them.

As Kim stood watching her friends walk away, Andrea drove into the driveway with one of her friends.

"I know you didn't have those tramps at my mother's house," she said, as she placed her hand on her hip.

"You don't know them. They're my friends," Kim replied.

"Oh, I know them. Those misfits are a bunch of losers. That Marissa got suspended from school last year. And that other one's parent sells drugs. I am telling my mother about this. We don't allow losers in our house. I hope she throws you out with your loser friends," Andrea announced, strutting past Kim and entering the house.

Kim sat down on the chair, shocked by Andrea's revelation. She didn't know whether to believe her or not. Her heart told her that her friends were good people, but would Allison believe her daughter over Kim? She wanted to go with Quaneisha tomorrow. Would Allison let her go? Her friend needed her support and you had to be there for your friends. But Allison had been so wonderful to her, and Kim felt obligated to this family. Suddenly she was uncertain whether she should ask for permission to go with her friend or keep quiet. Kim walked silently back into the house like a deflated balloon.

Chapter 9

Kim woke up the next morning, conflicted between supporting her friend and being honest with Allison. If Andrea had told her mother that her friends were bad news, then she would be banned from them. Andrea hadn't said anything else to her. Kim could not tell if she was bluffing or if she really had told her mother.

Kim was in a difficult position. She gave her word to Marissa and Quaneisha and it was important to her to stand by it. She knew there was nothing wrong with supporting a friend and they weren't going to do anything illegal. But she had to think of a way out of the house without lying and without jeopardizing her relationship with the family. Finally, she decided that she would leave a note.

She grabbed her blue sundress and silver flip-flops and headed to the bathroom to dress. Then she quickly made her bed and placed her folded pajamas on the end. When she finished dressing and straightening up, she scribbled a quick note to Allison: *I am headed to the mall with my friend Q so that she isn't alone on the bus.*

She knew it was a crazy note, but she would explain everything when she got back.

"Where are you going?" Andrea asked, as Kim reached toward the door leading into the room.

"None of your business," Kim answered, as she stepped around Andrea.

"We will see what my mother thinks about that," Andrea responded.

"We will see what she thinks about you stealing, too," Kim spat.

Andrea rolled her eyes and silently went into her room.

Kim walked through the kitchen and was heading out the front door when it opened.

"Good morning, Kim. Where are you headed so early?" Allison asked.

"Oh, hello. I was leaving you a note. I was headed to the park for a class, and then I wanted to catch some lunch with my friends from class," Kim spilled out.

"Alright, have fun," Allison responded.

A bead of sweat formed on Kim's forehead as she walked out the front door. She read her note and crumpled it. When she came face to face with Allison, the truth would not come out. As she walked down the street to meet Quaneisha, she felt caved in, her shoulders slumped her head down. She wanted to go back and tell the truth and let the chips fall. She owed the family so much more than lies.

Kim hated liars. Her father had lied to her so many times. She remembered him lying to her and

67

Kevin when he took them to a gambling place so he could drink and play cards with his friends. She and Kevin sat in a hot car baking all day while her father got drunk and gambled away the little bit of money he had.

How could she lie the same way he did? She could argue it was for the greater good, but no one benefitted from lies. This could damage the foundation of a budding relationship. This one lie could shatter her life. Plus, what would Kevin think? He brought her here and how did she repay him? With lies. She wanted to help her friend, but she shouldn't have lied to do it. Kim felt sick to her stomach, as she looked up to see Quaneisha waiting at the corner.

"Hey, girl, thanks again for taking the trip with me," Quaneisha said.

"It's cool," Kim answered.

"We'll take the shortcut through the park, so we can catch the bus on Skyline," Quaneisha replied.

As they walked through the park, Kim felt guilty hearing the music from the dance class drifting through the open gym door.

Quaneisha noticed Kim looking toward the open door. "Marissa went to class. She will show us the new moves later, okay?"

"Okay," Kim responded.

"Hey, what's wrong?" Quaneisha asked.

"I didn't tell Kevin's parents where I was going, and I feel bad about it," Kim replied.

"You want to call or go back? I'll understand if you do. I don't want you to get in trouble."

"No, I'm going with you. I want to go. It's just Andrea said some bad things about you guys, and she said she was going to tell her mother not to let me hang around you. She is such a… uhh." Kim sighed.

"What'd she say?" Quaneisha asked, as they

68

deposited their fare in the slot at the front of the bus.

"She said you both got suspended last year. She will make it sound like it was a federal offense, I'm sure."

"Well, I hit a bully for picking on a freshman because she had on holey clothes. He was some rich jerk; whose daddy bought his way out of a suspension. I would do it again. Damn anyone who wants to judge me."

"Like I said, I figured Andrea was full of crap. I just don't know if her mother realizes it. I think that what you did took a lot of courage."

Kim remembered the bully who hit her in school the previous year, and how humiliating it had been to walk around campus with a black eye.

"Well no one takes up for the misfits, and I refuse to let anyone walk all over me," Quaneisha responded.

Kim decided that when she got home, she would tell Allison the truth. In this case, the truth was good. And in any case, it was bad to lie.

Relieved with her decision, she sat back and thought about what Quaneisha said. No one took up for the misfits. She was a misfit and she knew what it meant to have no one take up for you. Kim remembered when she had holes in her pants and had to get on the bus. The kids were cruel and laughed at her, and the bully pushed Kim for no apparent reason. It still saddened Kim to think about how many times she had to wear old faded clothes that were too short or falling apart. After her mother died, they had no money for extra expenses, so she and Kevin wore what they had. Kim looked down at her blue sundress and felt guilty again. Kids could be cruel.

It took a little over an hour to reach the county jail out in Chula Vista. Quaneisha seemed to get quieter the closer they got to the jail.

"Will they let you see him without an adult?" Kim asked.

"My grandmother is here, so I should be able to get in. He wrote me and said he placed me on the list, and I brought everything he said I would need."

"I will meet you right here in two hours. Have a great visit, Q," Kim said, as she hugged her friend. "It will be alright. Don't worry."

Kim watched Quaneisha walk into the building, then turned and headed toward the bus stop to catch the bus to the mall. When she arrived at Plaza Bonita, she decided to go looking for a present for Allison, to thank her for all she had done. Then she decided to text Allison. "Change of plans at mall, will be home in few hours." Kim hit send.

Reassured, she headed toward Forever 21, where she picked up a pair of jeans shorts off the clearance rack. Kim took two sizes to the fitting room to try on. The size five fit perfectly. Her skin looked golden brown from the sunny days in California. Her almond eyes were smiling at the reflection. She had to buy the shorts; they fit all her curves.

Kim glanced at the price tag. It said 14.99. She had twenty dollars to spend from the money Allison gave her for the week. She took the shorts to the register.

"Today is your lucky day, you can get an additional 30% off today, because we are having a one-day sale. Your total is 10.99."

Kim paid the bill, took her shorts, and headed for another store. She grabbed a corn dog and lemonade on the way to H&M. She thought about all the times she had been hungry in Texas. She had been so naïve when it came to her father. He lied so many times, and she believed him. Kim thought about the many nights her father stayed out drinking and lied about it. Kim remembered arguing with Kevin about their dad. Kevin tried to tell her the truth about their dad being a drunk all the time, to convince her that his drinking was more important than the bills. Thinking about the pain her father was in over losing his wife, Kim had taken up for her dad and chose to look at him through rose- colored glasses. Kim made excuses for his flaws and forgave him when he lied. It was so hard to give up on someone you loved. Kevin made the decision that was best for his life. Now her father wanted her to trust in him and return to the life she escaped.

Kim continued walking through the mall. How could she believe her father? How could she ever trust in him? It had been so hard living alone, with no one to look out for her except her friends. Kim would have starved if she had not gotten a job and had friends who cared enough to feed her. Kim had to find out if her father was lying again. She wouldn't be a fool a second time; she'd demand solid proof that he was better. She stopped in Claire's accessory store and picked out a pair of silver hoop earrings for Allison.

Kim then headed in H&M and tried on several dresses, but the color wasn't right. There was nothing in her price range, so she headed back to the bus stop to catch the bus to meet up with Quaneisha.

Quaneisha sent a text saying she was on her way back to the bus and would join her so they could go home.

Kim glanced at her watch; it had only been an hour since they'd parted. She hoped everything went alright. It was a good thing Kim was here to support her friend. She knew firsthand how disappointing parents could be.

Twenty-minutes later, Quaneisha entered the

bus looking down. She glanced up once to locate Kim and then back toward the floor.

Kim noticed her red eyes and slow shuffle and reached for her friend's hand and squeezed it. Quaneisha squeezed back. Kim let her friend have her silence.

Quaneisha remained silent for a long time. Finally, she spoke.

"He needs me to bring him some medicine, because they don't give you medicine in jail." Then she looked out the window and said, "The messed-up part of the visit was that he only had fifteen minutes for me, because his two girlfriends were coming and he wanted to spend time with them."

"Couldn't one of his women have come on a different day, so that you guys could visit longer?" Kim asked.

"He said they both got rides today, and I could come back next Saturday with his medicine."

"What kind of medicine?" Kim asked.

"He said he needs medicinal marijuana and his friend Jay would bring it to me and explain where I was to drop it off." Quaneisha looked devastated, then continued. "He said he is so sick that he can't eat. He would never make it without his meds."

"I thought marijuana was illegal. Why would he ask you to do something that was illegal?" Kim asked.

"He said it was not illegal for people with medical marijuana cards."

"Well he should have asked his girlfriends to bring it to him since they are adults," Kim replied. "You should not do anything illegal for him. You could go to jail."

"He said it was not illegal. I asked if I could ask the police where to drop it off and he said they would keep it for themselves. He didn't ask about me or how I was doing. That is what bites. The whole fifteen minutes was about getting his medicine."

"What did you tell him?" Kim asked.

"I told him I would think about it, and he said kids should help out their parents. Family was a two-way street and all of that."

"He reminds me of my dad, always thinking about himself first. My dad's girlfriend got mad at him and he left me home alone for a few days to go fix things up with her," Kim confided. "I had no food in the house and the water had been turned off. He didn't call to check on me. I missed the school bus and he never knew. Q, don't let your dad get you into trouble."

Quaneisha looked out the window as they neared their stop. "I won't," she whispered. "I'll call you tomorrow. I don't feel like lunch today. Rain check, okay?"

Kim nodded.

Kim and Quaneisha separated at the hill and Kim headed home. Quaneisha's dad was a jerk and he sounded like he was lying to her. His story was full of holes. Kim wanted to help her friend navigate through the haze to the truth. It had been hard for Kim to see the truth about her dad; she just hoped Quaneisha didn't have to learn the hard way. Kim knew how hard it was hard to give up on parents, even when they were wrong

While she was walking, Kevin pulled up next to her. "Get in. I'll give you a ride."

"Thanks," she replied, as she got in the car.

"Where are you coming from?" he asked.

"I was helping a friend," she answered.

"She is lucky to have you. I am happy you are here, Kim. In case I haven't told you yet, I really missed you. I really want this to work out for you. Just please do me a favor."

"What is it?" Kim asked.

"Please think about the lies dad told us before you go back to that life. And talk to my parents out here. They're good people," Kevin pleaded, as he pulled in front of the house.

"I will," she responded. They walked up the driveway. Kim dropped her head. How could she have lied to Allison? Look what they had done for her. Her brother invited her into his family's home and she repaid him with lies. She was no better than her dad. She lied to the people who seemed to care about her well-being. Kevin was going to think she was as bad as their father.

When she walked into the house, Kim's stomach dropped as she saw Allison's expression. Andrea had a smug look on her face and that could only mean one thing. She told her mother about Kim's friends.

Kim headed straight to the bedroom to wait for the yelling to start.

Chapter 10

Kim sat on her bed, biting her nails. She could hear Kevin's parents talking in their room across the hall. She feared she had crossed a line and there was no going back; her lie had taken away any trust they had for her. She had let everyone down. She should just pack her bags.

Allison stepped out of her bedroom and walked over to Kim's doorway. "Kim, can you come follow me? We want to talk to you."

Kim hung her head and walked behind Allison to her bedroom.

Allison pointed to a desk chair. "Have a seat there," she said, taking a seat next to her husband.

Kim swallowed hard.

"We are disappointed in you for lying to us," Allison said. "You were not at the gym."

Kim almost lied and said yes, she was in the park, because that was technically the truth. They could have missed seeing her. It wasn't exactly a lie; it was partially true. They could ask Marissa, she wanted to insist. Marissa would tell them Kim was at the park.

But Kim looked up at the sadness on Allison's face and the lie froze on the end of her tongue. Then she looked up and saw an image of Francis sitting next to Allison, smiling, and Kim's past came flooding back to her. The many lies and deceits of her father came crashing down on her heart.

She remembered the day her father promised they would spend time together, but instead went gambling and drinking with his friends. He was never planning on spending the day with her and Kevin. He ended up spending the night in jail. They were so many lies she remembered her father telling her, that after a while, she rarely believed anything he said. The hurt and disappointment she bestowed on them was unbearable. How could she become her father? Kim cringed at the thought. She should know by now that one lie always leads to two. She couldn't bear to think she would hurt people by her lies the way Francis hurt her.

Kim slumped her shoulders, looked up at Allison and prepared to answer her questions. "No, I wasn't at the gym."

"Where were you?"

"My friend Quaneisha needed someone to go with her to Chula Vista on the bus and I volunteered. I didn't want her to go alone. She was going to see her father. I know I should have asked before I promised to go. I made the promise and I didn't want to let her down," Kim sputtered.

"I understand wanting to help a friend, but we don't lie in this house. We expect our children to be honest, and that includes you. You should have asked before you committed," Allison responded. "Now you will be grounded for two weeks, no phone, no dance class, nothing."

Kim's mouth fell open. She had never been grounded before. But Allison had said grounded, not pack your bags, so she had to be grateful that they weren't going to send her away. "I am sorry that I was not honest with you."

"How well do you know these friends?" Robert asked. He had been totally silent until then.

"We met at dance class. They are good people who have had a rough time, like me. They should not be blamed for who their parents are. Will you get to know them and then judge for yourself?" Kim asked.

"We will, but know this: who you associate with dictates the type of person you become. We won't allow you or any of our other kids to hang around delinquents."

"Fair enough," Kim responded, thinking that her friends weren't bad people. They'd just had hard lives, like she had in Texas. But they weren't delinquents.

"You may go, but remember it is always better to tell us the truth."

Kim stood up, lowered her head for the walk of shame out of their room. She felt a single tear slip down her cheek. She remembered, back in Texas, saving a sandwich from lunch to eat later, and the many times her friends fed her to keep her from starving. Kevin's parents provided everything Kim needed and she had broken their trust. This felt bad. Kim sat down on the bed; and her pink phone stared back at her, temping and taunting. She never had so many nice things, and now one lie could have ended it all. It was important to be there for her friends, but she had to do it without compromising her values. She had to listen to and respect Allison and Robert and their rules.

Before Kim could fully get her mind together, Kevin stormed into her room. "Kim, why did you do this to me? What were you thinking?" he seethed, throwing his hands in the air with frustration. He closed his eyes and shook his head.

"I am sorry. I was just trying to help my friend," Kim answered.

"Your friends don't live here. You do," Kevin said. "I should have mattered to you, not her. Me and the fact that I brought you here."

"You are my brother and I love you," Kim answered, her insides twisting. How did she get herself into such a mess? She hadn't meant to hurt her brother. He had to believe her. Lies did so much damage. Would he ever trust or forgive her? "I never meant to hurt you or your family."

"I don't know if I can trust you again," Kevin uttered.

"I know, just let me prove it to you. Andrea said she was going to tell Allison to ban me from seeing my friends and I already promised I would help Q out. I just didn't want to let her down. She has no family."

"Maybe you shouldn't hang out with her if you got to lie to do it. Friends don't ask you to lie."

"Kevin, she didn't know I lied. It is not her fault. I did it. I was trying to support her since she doesn't have anyone else."

"Obviously your friends mean more to you than I do. I risked my life for you, not them," he spat.

"I'm sorry. I didn't mean to hurt you. You're my brother. I love you."

"Save it, liar. You remind me of Francis. You

are turning into him," Kevin taunted.

"No, I am not," Kim said loudly, turning her head to hide the hurt and shame. Her brother struck a chord when he compared her to her dad. How could he be so cold? One lie and he was ready to throw her to the wolves. Kim stifled back her tears, refusing to cry. "At least he didn't up and leave me without letting me know he was okay!" Kim yelled. She regretted it the moment the words left her lips. "I didn't mean it," she said.

"Yes, you did. This was all the thanks I get, for getting my father to bring you here. Go back to Texas and live with that low-life you call dad. I tried to help you and I see it is not appreciated," Kevin said, and then stormed out of the room.

Kim couldn't hold the pain anymore. She started shaking and crying. Her brother was all she had left and now he hated her. She should go back to Texas; she deserved to live in that turmoil she left there. Her dreams had been so important, and now they seemed like fairy tales. How was she going to go to college? She made a mistake and now all her hopes and dreams would be shattered. Kim wiped her runny nose on her sleeve and crawled into a ball on her bed.

Andrea walked in the room singing to her iPod. The day was getting worse and worse.

Kim ignored her, staring at the wall. She wondered if Andrea told her mother about her going with Quaneisha? Asking Andrea directly was not an option, though she strongly suspected Andrea opened her big mouth.

Suddenly Andrea cleared her throat. "Riding buses with criminals, next thing you know you'll be transporting drugs,' Andrea taunted. 'I'll have my room back in no time."

"Stealing is illegal too, so maybe you'll be the

one going to jail," Kim spat.

Andrea didn't think her stealing was wrong, but she quickly pointed out faults in others. Andrea just revealed her part in Kim getting busted. How could one person be so mean?

"Whatever. Don't let me bother you, since you will be stuck in here for, what was it? Two weeks?" Andrea said, as holding up two fingers.

Kim sucked in a breath and bit her lip, resisting the urge to punch Andrea in that mouth of hers. The only thing Kim did to this girl was exist in her space, and Andrea had continually been a jerk about it. Kim focused on trying to remain calm. The best way to win this battle was to keep cool. She knew Andrea's parents would surely send Kim packing if she attacked their precious daughter.

"Maybe you can go live with your hoodlum friends in their group home. Kevin is even getting sick of you being here anyway."

Kim turned around and sat up on the bed. "Kevin and I will discuss our relationship. That's not your business. As for you, you can't stand the fact that you are not the center of attention, and that's pathetic. Those fake, plastic people you surround yourself with are the real trash." Kim feelings were hurt. Bringing up Kevin pushed at the bottled-up pain from his earlier yelling spree. Her friends' values were being attacked too, and they were innocent. How could she have known one lie would produce so much harm?

Kim went in the bathroom and started running water for a bath. Because she was grounded, she couldn't go for a run to release the tension. She figured that maybe a hot bath would help. She heard the music fading down the hall and knew Andrea left too. Kim stepped into the hot water and sank into the tub. It had been a long day. She shouldn't have lied.

Now everyone was disappointed in her. It hurt most that Kevin was so angry. Never would she have wanted to jeopardize his relationship with his parents.

Kim also felt bad about Quaneisha. She wanted to be there for her friend, and now she was grounded. How was she going to convince Quaneisha not to take drugs into jail for her father? Andrea was right about that; carrying any type of drugs could lead to serious trouble. Kim learned in Texas that friends didn't leave you out in the cold. They feed you when you are hungry and give you rides when you are walking. Friends don't let each other down. She would talk to Q, no matter what.

Chapter 11

Kim opened her eyes and glared at the clock. It was two in the morning, ten days since her punishment began. The previous night, it had been hard for her to fall asleep. Kevin walked past her without speaking and the distance between them was breaking her heart. She could hear light snoring coming from the bed above her. Andrea slept peacefully, while Kim felt out of place and alone. She was in a house of strangers, and now she had alienated her brother, the only one who loved her. She tried to drift back off to sleep, but her eyelids kept popping back open.

Kevin would be leaving for work soon. Kim's heart ached to go talk to him. The thought that he was upset with her felt like a storm roaring through her bones. She knew it would have to run its course, but getting through it was hard. He thought she was a liar like Francis. Being compared to a drunk was very harsh and Kim couldn't shake the pain of those words. She hoped Kevin would give her another chance to prove herself worthy of staying in his house.

Kim watched the sunlight sneaking through the windows, but soon grew restless so she got up and headed for the bathroom. Allison was leaving her bedroom at the same time and smiled warmly.

"Good morning, Kim. Come help me with breakfast after you get out of the bathroom," she said.

"Okay," Kim said.

Fear grabbed Kim and held her hostage. Allison didn't act like she hated her. Was this a cruel joke? Would she berate her during breakfast? Was this how people reacted normally? Surely, she was dreaming. Kim took a deep breath and walked the long mile to the kitchen.

"There you are. Peel ten potatoes for me, would you?" Allison asked.

Kim nodded, washed her hands again even though she'd just left the bathroom, and began silently peeling the potatoes.

"Before you peel, you should rinse them off. Do you know how to cut up potatoes?" Allison asked.

"No," Kim answered.

Allison took one potato and demonstrated how to cut it up, then handed the knife to Kim to finish the job.

"Tell me something. Do you miss your friends in Texas?" Allison inquired.

"Yeah," Kim answered softly.

"It's hard coming to a new place and starting a new life." Allison talked while she beat the eggs. "We are happy you came and I want you to come to me with any questions or concerns. I want to make your transition an easy one, you know."

"You aren't mad at me?" Kim asked.

Allison appeared calm, like a loving parent. It made talking to her welcoming and easy.

"No, I'm not mad. All kids make mistakes, Kim. All kids. We want ours to learn from them and make better decisions the next time. You have received your punishment, and that is the end of it. The rules are the same for all of you." She smiled at Kim.

"Thank you," Kim responded, relieved. She had been so sure that Allison was angry, but Allison was being so reasonable, just like Maggie had been. Maggie never got angry. She approached every situation with love and wisdom.

"I usually have the kids read ten books over the summer so that they aren't stale in the fall. We have a small library in the family room; I'd like you to pick out a book to read so that you can join in."

"Cool," Kim said. "I like reading."

"Oh yeah?" Allison asked, grinning. "What is the last book you read?"

"I haven't really read much since school ended, but I liked reading at school."

"Okay, good. Then you'll enjoy your reading this summer. Now please butter the toast so we can have breakfast."

"Thank you again," Kim said.

"No worries, honey."

Kim felt ashamed that she lied. Everything they did had been fair, and they were treating her like their own daughter.

Kim placed the food on the table, then ate her breakfast in silence as everyone talked about what they would be doing over the coming week. Julian had Pop Warner football practice and Andrea had cheer practice.

Kevin ate quickly and left for work, looking around the table to gauge the mood. Kim wanted to stop him and talk to him, but she didn't know what to say. He had been so angry the other night. The friction between them was thick as fog, and Kim had no idea how to get him to listen to her. The pain tore through her when Kevin left Texas, and now it felt like the wound was reopening. How could she cause so much turmoil between them? This was the hardest part of breaking the house rules: disappointing her brother.

Kim helped wash the dishes and dry, while Julian put the dishes away. When they finished, Kim headed toward her the room, but stopped when Allison spoke.

"Hey Kim, don't forget to pick out a book from the library in the family room."

"Okay, I will," Kim responded.

She headed to the bookshelf to look at the titles. The shelves were full. Kim read excerpts from a few books. The main genre seemed to be fantasy, which was fine with her even though she usually enjoyed mysteries too.

She hadn't read Harry Potter like the rest of the kids. She took down Harry Potter and the Sorcerer's Stone and turned to go back to her room. With a good book, maybe the days would go by easier.

Just as she got to her room, the pink phone on her bed buzzed, indicating a new text message. Kim tapped the "on" button by mistake when she picked the phone up off the nightstand. "Sorry you are on lock down and we missed you at dance class," Marissa's message read. "We will catch you up when you come back. Q feels bad you got in trouble."

Kim felt guilty for reading the screen. Allison trusted her enough to let her keep the phone through her punishment. Till then, she hadn't broken any rules of her grounding since she'd once she sent a quick text to Marissa before her punishment was handed down. But now she had crossed another line and read a message. She couldn't feel totally guilty, though, as she was more concerned about Quaneisha's predicament.

I told the lie, not Q. She shouldn't blame herself, Kim thought.

She wondered if Quaneisha had made her decision yet. And if she had, Kim hoped it would be the right decision. What her father asked her to do felt wrong. Hopefully Kim would have time to talk her friend out of making a big mistake.

The phone buzzed again.

"Kim, my dad's friend says it's cool to help my dad," Quaneisha's text read. "Sorry 'bout the lock down."

No, Q had to wait, Kim thought. She can't go before I talk to her. What kind of adult sends a child into prison? They had to be shady people to use kids.

Kim was determined to uncover all the facts for her friend. But she was on restriction. How could she get the information to Quaneisha?

Another text from Quaneisha came through. "Don't worry, it will be fine."

Kim shook her phone in frustration. She could have screamed.

Kim grabbed her laptop and Googled items that can legally be brought into a jail. She learned that all items have to be mailed to the inmate so that everything can be inspected. Then the inmates are given items that are on the approved list.

Kim looked down the approved lists of items. Medical marijuana was not listed. In fact, the article said it was a felony to bring any kind of drugs into a prison. She closed the laptop and walked back to her room. It had been so simple to find the truth, and she had to share it with Quaneisha. Quaneisha's father asked her to do something illegal. Did he even care if she went to jail? Kim wondered.

Squeezing her fists, Kim thought about Francis and how he constantly lied to her. She remembered how easy it was to believe your parents and how hard it might be to convince Quaneisha not to help her father. Kim thought about how Francis lied about stealing money that Kevin made as a kid mowing lawns. Kim waited up for her father at night when he stayed out all night drinking. When adults use drugs or alcohol, they care more about getting high than they about their kids. Kim was furious at Quaneisha's dad and his friend. Her dad's friend didn't want to take the risk so they asked a kid to do it. Quaneishia's future didn't matter, and now she could go to jail for trying to help her father.

Kim still had three more days of her restriction and she was dying to warn her friend. Maybe she could risk texting Quaneisha. But did she want to risk Robert and Allison's disappointment? Would they understand her reasoning? It was a life-or-death situation. And anyway, they would probably never know, Kim reasoned. But then she realized, if they looked at her phone, she would be forced in a corner and be faced with telling them that she had broken her punishment.

What about Kevin? Would this sever their relationship, which was already on rocky ground? He would probably hate her for disappointing his parents a second time but this was her friend's life. The benefits outweighed the risks. You had to help your friends. Maybe she could ask Kevin to send a text to Quaneisha. He could buy some time, and then Kim could show her the facts. No one wanted to willingly go to jail. You can still save her, Kim thought to herself.

Kim settled down on the bed to read her book. She read until dinnertime. Escaping to the world of Hogwarts brightened her mood. Harry found some good friends at school, just like Kim's friends. He stuck by his friends like Kim was trying to do for hers. She was going to talk to her brother after dinner, she decided, and hopefully this would solve two problems at once, because she would ask Kevin to text her friend the truth. He would help her because he hated liars.

Kim ate dinner in silence, building her courage with each bite of food. She could do it. She could do it.

"Kevin, can we talk?" Kim asked softly as they were finishing the meal.

"Tomorrow when I'm off. I am headed out tonight," Kevin answered.

Deflated, Kim nodded, trying to hide her disappointment. Her voice would crack if she spoke. She lowered her head and headed to bed. Breathing deeply, she calmed herself down. Tomorrow would be soon enough to fix her problems. It would be ok, she would tell Quaneisha tomorrow. It had to work, oh please let it work out, Kim prayed as she lay down to sleep.

Her phone buzzed. *I am going to c my dad tomorrow. -Q.*

Chapter 12

Kim waited up trying to talk to Allison for as long as her body would allow, and now a cold panic woke her. Kim needed to talk to Quaneisha immediately. She leapt from the bed and threw open the door, but when she knocked on Allison's door, she was greeted by an eerie silence.

Quaneisha's last text meant Kim was quickly running out of time to keep her from taking drugs into the prison for her dad. Kim had only a few more hours to stop her friend from making a terrible mistake. Kevin had to be awake now; she needed him to listen to what she had to say. Marching back to her brother's room, Kim knocked.

No answer. She knocked again. Silence.

"Where is everybody?" Kim asked herself.

Kim headed to the kitchen to search for

someone to help her; then she saw a shadow pass on the outside patio: Kevin. Relief flooded her as she marched to the door leading outside, willing to face his disappointment and anger. He looked up, puzzled by her haste and motioned for her to sit down. What is Kevin doing?

"I know you are disappointed in me, and I am sorry," Kim blurted out. "We all make mistakes."

Kevin looked up and nodded.

"I hope you can forgive me. You are all that I have. And I love you," Kim said, as she sat on the edge of the cold patio chair across from her brother. "I forgave you," she whispered, allowing the words to float between them.

Kim remembered looking everywhere for Kevin when he ran away from home and how the police volunteer took her out for days searching all over for her brother. She had been worried for months, not knowing what happened to her brother, who left Texas without saying anything, to live with his family in California.

Hurt and shame flickered across Kevin's face. He glanced down, then looked at his sister, "I'm sorry." He reached over the table and grabbed Kim's hands and squeezed. "I never meant to hurt you. I needed to get out and I didn't think you would leave."

"I know it was hard," Kim replied. She remembered sitting at home in the dark after Kevin left. Her father stopped paying the rent and the utilities, spending all his money on liquor and gambling. She remembered the many nights she didn't know if she would have food to eat because her father did not come home.

Tears slipped down Kevin's cheeks. "I am so sorry."

"I made a mistake," Kim continued. "My mistake not yours. I am sorry if you feel it made you look bad, but I am not perfect. I can never live up to that standard, so maybe I should leave. When I was alone in Texas, at least I thought I had you as my brother, even though you weren't there," Kim revealed.

"I was worried my real father would put us out for your mistakes, but that was totally stupid," Kevin replied. "I was disappointed, but I never stopped to hear your side of the story. Now who is acting like Francis?"

"I had to try and help my friends. They are good kids, struggling like us to survive without parents," Kim said. "They need a family too."

"We have a family now," Kevin replied.

"They don't, and I can't turn my back on friends in need. Quaneisha needed someone to go with her to go visit her father. Turns out he is a low life."

Kim knew she had Kevin's attention then. The anger faded from his body and he was leaning forward into the conversation.

"She is still fooled by her father, just like I was by Francis. I wanted to see the good in Francis because he had not always been bad."

"I know, but I don't think kids should have to endure some things, like alcoholism or drugs," Kevin responded.

"You're right. It took me longer to realize that. I know to look deeper before I believe him now. But my friend is still blinded by her father. She asked for my help and I didn't want to abandon her when she needed me."

"I can respect that," Kevin acknowledged.

"The trouble is, she still needs me. Even more. Her dad has asked her to bring marijuana into the prison. He has her convinced that he needs it medically and it is safe to bring it in. He doesn't care about ruining her life. He is selfish and doesn't care whom he hurts," Kim told Kevin.

"How can we help her?" Kevin asked.

"I don't think she knows how much trouble she can get in for what she's about to do. I need to warn her that it is illegal to carry any kind of drugs into a prison. Would you text her for me?" Kim asked. "I don't want to break any rules of my punishment."

"What is her number?" Kevin asked, then he punched in the numbers on his phone. "This is Kim's brother. Don't take anything into your visit. It is against the law and punishable with jail time," he wrote.

"Tell her I will call her in a few days," Kim interjected.

"Kim will call you when she gets off punishment," Kevin continued the text to Quaneisha.

"Kim, I hope she listens because I have seen women on the news being sent to jail for being caught transporting drugs into prison. I hate men like her father," Kevin said, making a fist.

"It makes me angry, too. I don't understand how a parent could put their child in danger. They are supposed to protect us," Kim admonished.

"I hope your message helps," Kevin replied.

"Thanks, me too."

Kim really hoped Quaneisha got the message. Her friend was in danger, but it was out of her hands now. There was not anything else that could be done. Kim still felt bad because she was not able to talk to her friend directly. Kevin had come through for her when she needed him. There was hope for their relationship.

"Kim, your friend had to know her father is asking her to do something wrong."

"She believes he wouldn't ask her to do

anything illegal. How can adults lie to their kids?" Kim asked her brother.

"That is why I left Texas. When Francis stole the money from our inheritance, I was disappointed. But when he took my money that I went out and earned, I was done. You should be able to trust your parents. I could never live with him again," Kevin responded.

Kim knew Kevin was right about their father. Maggie left money for them to use for college and their father petitioned the courts for access to pay the bills. When the courts gave Francis the money, he did pay the bills for a while, but it wasn't long before he couldn't keep the bills current. It had been a nightmare. Kim became the parent and her father was like the child. No child should have to live life like that. She wanted to spare Quaneisha the same disappointment.

"I will try to listen before I judge in the future. My dad talked to me. He told me that you had to feel lonely being here with strangers and I needed to be supportive. He also said he would never give me up," Kevin responded. He stood and opened his arms. "I was a jerk."

Kim jumped into her brother's arms, her body shaking with the pent-up pain and tears. She cried for the loneliness she felt, the father she loved and missed, and the friend she hoped was safe. Until Kevin confirmed her feelings, Kim was content denying she felt anything. But what Kevin said was right. It was hard living with complete strangers and failing to fit in. Kevin was home, and he had a family who loved him. She couldn't even get along with her roommate, Andrea.

When her only ally turned against her, the world felt dark. She felt as lonely as she felt in Texas when Kevin left her, only this time he was physically present.   Family was important and Kim never wanted to lose her brother's love.

"Hey silly. It's okay, don't cry. I didn't mean to make you cry."

Kim couldn't form the words. She squeezed her brother tighter.

He saw the pain on her face. "I am not leaving you, okay?" he whispered. "I am so sorry I left you there. I didn't mean to hurt you."

"I know," Kim said. She wiped her eyes with the back of her hands. "I don't feel at home here."

"I don't understand." Kevin said, releasing Kim while still holding her hand.

"I just feel like the outsider."

"I should have spent more time with you. Everyone is happy to have you here. It has just been a busy summer. From now on, I am going to make sure you and I have time together.

"No, everyone is not happy to have me here. Did anyone ask Andrea if she wanted a roommate, because she does not want me here," Kim replied. "I get it and I don't blame her. It is just hard to live with her."

"I didn't know it was that bad."

"Do you ever see us talking or hanging out?"

Kevin shook his head.

"This is her world and her family. I am the outsider," Kim responded. "I don't know how long I can live like this. Then you turned against me too."

"I didn't think of it that way. I just thought you would melt into the family. I haven't helped much with your transition. I am going to help you find a solution to the problem between you and Andrea."

Kim smiled for the first time all week. She did not feel as alone anymore.

Chapter 13

K im was excited. This afternoon was the big party. Her punishment was over and she was ready to let her hair down, check out the scenery, and listen to some good music. Kevin spent time with her the last few days of her confinement. It was great to have him back in her life again.

All the kids had been assigned a Saturday to cook breakfast, allowing Allison the time to rest. It was Kim's turn to cook. Pancakes were on the menu, and Kim wanted to make sure they tasted good. The recipe was so simple: just add water.

Spraying the griddle, she allowed it to get hot while she stirred the batter. Placing a pan of bacon in the oven to cook, she started pouring the pancakes on the griddle. When the holes formed, Kim flipped the golden brown, fluffy pancakes.

The smell of bacon filled the kitchen. Maggie cooked breakfast for them every morning until she got sick. Smiling, Kim remembered the family she once had, the love her mother poured into everything she did, and how happy Maggie appeared when she cooked. Kim set the table and placed the pile of bacon and platter of pancakes in the center. "Breakfast is ready!" she yelled.

Julian, Kevin, and Mark were the first to emerge from their rooms, then Allison and Robert, followed by Andrea entered the dining room. "Good morning," Kevin's parents said.

Everyone replied. The blessings were given and the pancakes started evaporating from the serving dish. "This is good, Kim," Kevin said between chewing.

"Yeah, it is good," Allison chimed in.

"Thanks, I learned from watching my mother. She was an excellent cook," Kim replied. Once again Maggie's warmth filled Kim's heart. She would be proud to see Kim now. Family was so important to her mother. Kim and Kevin were together again.

"I hear she was a great woman. I am so thankful that she loved our Kevin while he was in her care," Allison replied.

"Yeah, she was a great woman," Kim whispered. Sadness crept into her, and she looked down to avoid showing the pain this conversation evoked. She wanted someone to change the subject. The loss of her mother left a hole that was never filled. The pain was still fresh.

Kim took a bite of her pancake and glanced around the table. Andrea was picking at her food, looking like a lost puppy, and she remained quiet through the whole meal. This was odd behavior for her since she always had something to say. After all, she knew everything.

Allison took charge of the conversation again. "Are you looking forward to the pool party?"

"Yes, it will be my first pool party," Kim responded, relieved.

"I am sure you will have fun. The Johnsons have only lived here for a year, but they have been a welcome addition to the neighborhood. Their son seems really nice," Allison said.

Andrea looked at her mother, disappointment flashing across her face for a quick second, before she hid it behind a glass of milk. It was odd to see Andrea looking less confident and sad. She seemed almost human. The vulnerability showed through her eyes. Kim resisted the urge to ask her what was wrong. Could she be disappointed about not being invited to the party?

"Are you okay?" Allison asked Andrea.

"Yeah, I'm fine," Andrea answered, with a false smile on her face.

Kim couldn't help wanting to cheer Andrea up. This was a side of Andrea that Kim found vulnerable and approachable. She made a mental note to remember this moment; it must be the side her brother saw.

Andrea glanced at Kim and frowned. Kim smiled. The old Andrea was back.

"What are you doing today?" her mother asked.

"I'll be home," Andrea answered.

Everyone cleared the table. Julian and Mark had kitchen duty, so Kim headed toward her room. She wanted to call Quaneisha. When she passed Kevin's room, she noticed he was pulling some shorts out of his dresser. She tapped on the door lightly.

"Got a minute?" Kim asked.

"Yeah, come in," Kevin answered. "I was

going to come talk to you in a minute anyway. Be ready by two. The party starts at one."

"I was thinking maybe you should take Andrea instead of me. She probably knows more people there. I am sure she would enjoy it," Kim responded.

"I am sure she can come too. He invited you, so you should go. I want you to meet some of my friends. Wait, let me text Davion."

Kevin grabbed his phone and sent a quick text. His phone chimed two seconds later.

"Andrea can come too," Kevin responded.

"Great, you ask her," Kim said.

"Maybe you should ask her. This might be a chance for you to get closer."

"It would be better coming from you," Kim responded.

"Andrea!" Kevin yelled.

Andrea walked into his room. "What's up?"

"Got a text from Davion inviting you to the party. You want to go with us?" he asked.

"Sure," she answered, smiling widely.

"We are leaving at two. Clear it with mom."

Andrea left the room, shoulders lifted, confidence back in her stride as she sauntered toward her bedroom. Kim had been right. Andrea wanted to go to the party. She would thrive in any event with the popular kids.

Kim walked in the room smiling. It had to be a disappointment not to be invited to the party of the summer.

Kim grabbed her phone and called Quaneisha. The phone continued to ring, then went to voice mail. "I am off punishment, call me," Kim responded into the phone.

Then she dialed Marissa's phone, which went directly to voice mail, where she left the same message.

Where were they? She checked the time and changed into her running sweats. It would take ten minutes to get to their house. She looked at Andrea as she left the room, hoping this would be the beginning of a truce between them.

Kim inhaled deeply as the fresh air hit her face. It was great to be outside again. She would go for a quick run, clear her head, and check on her friends. Kim ran down the path, toward the street. She was a little nervous to go to the party, where she didn't know anyone. Kevin was the only person there who would talk to her.

She made it to the corner of Noeline Lane and headed toward Noeline Avenue. As she rounded the corner, Davion ran toward her. When he smiled, her heart skipped a beat. Chocolate never looked so delicious. He was too gorgeous to notice a country girl like her.

"Hey! Kim, right?" Davion asked.

"Yeah, "she answered.

"How far are you running?" he asked.

"To the top of the hill and back down," Kim answered. She couldn't think of anything to say. She looked up at him, warming into the confidence he gave off.

"Can I run with you?" he asked.

Kim nodded, and they started running up the hill together.

"I enjoy running, it clears my head," Davion said after a few meters. "I wanted to have a few friends over to swim and my mom has turned this into a huge event. I don't like big crowds, but mom is determined to change that."

They ran by Quaneisha's house and Kim stopped. The house looked empty; even the van was gone from the driveway. Where could they all be?

She hoped nothing was wrong, but she had no choice but to wait for one of her friends to return her call. She and Davion reached the top of the hill, then turned and headed back down. They ran quietly, Kim turned toward her friends' house again as they passed it for the second time. It looked abandoned; maybe they were out babysitting. It was Saturday and people did need sitters on the weekend. Her friends would call back, she reminded herself as she and Davion jogged up their street toward the house.

"Thanks for the run. Are you always so quiet?" he asked.

"No, I am just worried about my friends. See, I have been on lock down for two weeks. My friend was a on the verge of doing something really stupid and I really hope she didn't do it."

"You can only give your friends advice. They have the responsibility of making the decision. Don't beat yourself up about it. I am sure you did your best," he responded.

"Thanks, I needed that," Kim said. "I am looking forward to going to your party later."

"I am happy to hear it. I was dreading it, but now it looks like it will be more interesting," Davion said with a grin. "See you later!"

Kim waved as she headed in the house, skipping. She felt better. Davion was right. She sent the text to her friend. It was Quaneisha's job to take the information and make the right the decision. Kim headed for the shower, confident her friends would call soon and she could tell them about her neighbor, sexy chocolate, Davion, and his pool party.

Chapter 14

Kim was excited and a little scared of being around a lot of people she didn't know. The last party she went to in Texas was fun, but ended badly. Kim remembered the guy she thought was so sweet trying to force her into sex before she was ready and lying about it to his friends. She would not make that mistake again.

Kim took out the strapless powder-blue one-piece swimsuit, and laid it on the bed, with the white cotton mini sundress and a pair of white flip-flops. The ironing board was still up. Kim looked over at Andrea as she walked into the room and grabbed her clothes for the shower. "Can I use the iron?" Kim asked, holding her breath. She didn't want Andrea to spoil her mood.

"Sure, I'm done," Andrea said, as she left the

room.

Kim grabbed the white knit sundress and ironed it. She was shocked by the pleasant tone of Andrea's response. She put the iron away, grabbed her swimsuit and headed for the bathroom as Andrea exited. Kim washed her hair, letting some of the hot water ease the nervousness. She pulled her loose curls up in a ponytail, put lotion on her legs, and pulled on her swimsuit. When she looked in the mirror, what she saw made her happy.

"Time to go!" Kevin yelled up the stairs.

Kim looked in the mirror one last time, "Coming!" she yelled back, putting on a little lip gloss.

Andrea walked out of the room, dressed in a fitted, short, pink-and-white dress and low heels. She placed her sunglasses on her head, her straight flat-ironed hair pulled back in a ponytail. Kim followed her brother and Andrea out the side door, a mixture of emotions rolling through her. Would she fit into this new crowd? Would they all be like Andrea or like her other friends? There were only three people she knew at this party. Did they do the same dances she knew? Was she overdressed? Looking at the two-piece pink bikini that peeked through Andrea's shear coverall, Kim wondered if this was the way girls dressed in California.

Rick Ross's "All I Do Is Win" was playing as they entered the backyard, which looked like a paradise. The pool was in the center, with a boulder fountain at the far end and palm trees strategically located around the back. There were small round tables with chairs all around the yard, covered with alternating blue and white tablecloths. The backyard was full, with kids dancing, sunbathing, and swimming. The three of them headed for the table where Kevin's girlfriend, Elise, sat waving to them.

"Kevin...over here!" she yelled. "I got the last

table."

"Hey, babe, you remember Andrea." Kevin kissed her and pointed "And this is my other sister, Kim."

"Hello, I am glad we get to hang out," Elise said.

"He should bring you by more often," Andrea said.

"Nice meeting you," Kim said.

Kim watched the exchange in awe. They were all talking back and forth like old friends, with nothing like the hostility that she received from Andrea. She felt a twinge of jealousy. Andrea was showing a human side. Kim felt like the person she was watching was an alien who switched places with the original. How could you get this person to permanently inhabit her body? Maybe Andrea would be nice to her from now on; this might be the turning point for their relationship.

Then Kim spotted Davion over by the food table talking to a group of guys. He had on a pair of blue board shorts with a Hawaiian print. The shorts hugged his slim waist, as the water from the pool glistened on his chest. He glanced Kim's way, smiled, and started walking toward their table. Kim hoped he had not seen her staring at him. She was accustomed to the way jocks behaved, and by the number of half-naked girls at the party, Davion fit the profile. Popular and gorgeous, he could have his pick of any girl at the party. Three different girls stopped him since he started walking in the direction of their table. Kim wondered what type of girl he dated: the cheerleader or the athlete? Then she shook her head and turned attention toward their table, where Andrea had removed her cover-up and stood with her hand on her hips, shoulders back, as if she were posing for a photograph.

"Hey guys, thanks for coming," Davion said, as he grabbed Kevin's hand for a quick man-hug.

"Thanks for inviting us," Andrea replied. "It looks like a great party. Everyone who is anybody is here."

"Yeah, I got a nice turnout," Davion said, looking around. "You guys need to get something to eat. My step-dad threw down with the chicken and ribs."

"We'll go get something to eat in a minute. Man, your mom went all out with the decorations."

"Yeah, she loves to have parties," Davion replied.

"Davion, are you playing basketball this year?" Andrea asked.

"Haven't decided yet," he replied politely and turned away from her. "Hey Kim, did you hear from your friend?"

"Not yet," Kim answered.

"I am sure you will soon."

"We're getting in the pool," Kevin said, as he took Elise's hand.

"Davion, come help me!" his mother yelled.

"I'll be back," he said.

Andrea smiled. "Okay."

"See that girl in the yellow polka dot bikini. She's the varsity cheerleading captain. This is gonna be the best party of the summer," Andrea said. "I can already tell."

Kim nodded, shocked by the fact that Andrea was having a conversation with her. She was being nice. This was the start of great times. It would be so nice to discuss things with her. Kim never had a sister, but now it was looking like she would get one. Kim smiled at Andrea. "I'm happy we came."

"Hey, I see some friends from school. I'll be back," Andrea said.

Kim sat down in the lounge chair. Great! She was all alone at the party of the summer. Her one-piece swimsuit looked out of place, and so did she. Watching the laughter and dancing reminded her of the friends she had back in Texas. They would spend the summer playing softball at the park down the street from her old house. She knew everyone there and felt comfortable hanging with her friends.

Cindy had been her best friend in Texas. They cheered on the freshman squad together. She missed her and the other friends she made, especially Keith, who came along at a tough time in her life.

Sitting all by herself and feeling uncomfortable, Kim looked around the backyard at the skimpy outfits, feeling overdressed.

She looked through her bag. No cell phone; she must have left it at home and Quaneisha might be trying to reach her. Kim decided to leave. She made an appearance at the party, and no one would miss her if she slipped away. After she got home, she would text Kevin. It was silly to think the popular kids wanted to meet her or get to know a girl from the country.

Kim gathered her bag and headed for the gate, when a hand touched her shoulder. As she turned and saw Davion, a tiny electrical current traveled through her body.

"Hey, where are you headed?" he asked.

"I was headed back home," she answered.

"Home?"

"Yeah, this is nice and all, but I really don't feel like partying."

"Cool, but I was hoping we could talk a little," he told her. "You think you could hang with me just a little while longer?"

"You have a whole backyard full of people. You don't need me."

"I want to get to know you better, Kim. I remember how it was for me last summer. No one wanted to hang out with me then," he said. "Come on, let me show you something."

Kim followed Davion through the sliding glass door as he walked through the kitchen. "Mom, this is Kim, Kevin's sister. I want to show her something. We will be right back."

"Hello, Kim, nice to me you," Davion's mother said.

"Hello, nice to meet you, too."

"Have you eaten, honey? Get some food when you guys come back through."

"Thanks, I'll make sure I do" Kim said.

"This is our family room," Davion said, pointing. "And this is my dad." Davion handed Kim a picture of a younger version of himself next to mature man. "He was killed in Iraq two years ago. My mother remarried and we moved here last summer. The only reason that backyard is full now is because I played football last season."

"You have made a lot of friends."

"A few, like your brother, are cool people, but the rest are pretty shallow. I could care less about being popular. It is more important to uphold the promise that I made to my dad: finish high school and go to college."

"My mother wanted me to go to college, too," Kim replied.

"I felt a connection to you when we met at your house. I really would like the chance to get to know you better," Davion said.

Kim looked up and saw sincerity in his eyes that were a totally gorgeous shade of light brown. He was too cute to want anything except friendship. Like Keith and Tim, cute men always saw her as a good friend. He probably thought she could be a good ear to listen to about his conquests and issues. There was no way he was interested in her. Yeah friendship was what he wanted from her. It was foolish to hope for anything more.

"Okay, I will stay for a little while longer."

"Good," Davion replied with a sigh. "What do you do for fun?"

"I run, read, and love dancing…that's about it."

Davion grabbed one of Kim's curls and twisted it around his finger. "You are so beautiful, you know. I love your curls."

Kim looked up into his gentle brown eyes, unable to speak. Mr. Gorgeous Popular Football Player was touching her hair. Kim shook from the chill that went down her spine. Would he want more than she was willing to give? Would he spread her name around his friends? Did she dare trust him?

"Come on, let's get some food and enjoy the party," Davion urged, pulling her up from the couch by her hand. He smiled as their bodies came inches apart. He led her back out to the kitchen, where two plates sat covered on the counter. They sat down and ate the ribs and baked beans. "My mom can really throw down in the kitchen."

Kim nodded in agreement. The food was wonderful. Her heart continued its rapid beat as she sat next to her new friend.

"Do you swim?" he asked.

"Not really. I don't know how," Kim answered.

"I can teach you if you like. I was a lifeguard in our old neighborhood."

"I would like that," Kim replied. When they finished their food, Davion again led Kim by the hand outside.

"Come meet some of the guys. Bo, Jerry,

Kyle, and Tom, this is Kim, Kevin's sister. She just moved here from Texas," he informed them.

"Nice to meet you," the guys replied in unison.

"Nice to meet you guys too," Kim replied.

"Come on, I want to show you something," Davion said, as he pulled her hand and walked toward the pool. "We can start your lessons as soon as you are ready."

"Let me check with Kevin's parents first," Kim replied.

"Cool. His parents, not yours?" he asked.

"Long story, but Kevin and I were both adopted to a family and our adoptive mother passed away. Kevin left and now he lives with his biological parents. I came to visit for the summer."

"What a story! Will you stay past the summer?"

"I don't know. My adoptive father wants me to come home."

"Well, I hope you stay."

"Thanks, Davion," Kim said.

"Call me D."

Kim giggled. "Alright, D."

Kim and Davion walked past Andrea and a group of her friends. Andrea stopped talking mid-sentence, frowned, and rolled her eyes. Kim wondered what the problem was now, but her attention was quickly pulled back to Davion, as he tugged her toward the shallow end of the pool.

"Wait, D, I thought the lesson would start next week," Kim said, trying not to sound panicked.

"Don't worry, no swimming today. We are just getting in the Jacuzzi," he replied, leading down the steps to sit in the Jacuzzi.

Kim enjoyed the warm water. The bubbles seemed to ease some of the tension in her body.

Kevin and Elise joined them.

"Kim, your phone has been buzzing in your bag," Kevin said before turning to Davion. "Great party, man."

"I thought I left it at home. Please excuse me," Kim replied, as she exited the Jacuzzi and made a dash for her bag. Her heart was throbbing in her chest. She hoped it was Quaneisha.

"Meet me at the park at six," Marissa texted.

"Okay," Kim texted back.

"Is everything okay?" Davion asked as he walked up behind her.

"Yeah, but I've gotta go. Thanks, D. I had fun."

"Me too," he replied. He took her phone and dialed his number. "Now you have my number. You should call."

"I will." As she walked out of the backyard she shouted. "Tell my brother I will see him at home!"

Kim headed to the park to meet with Marissa. She would finally find out what happened with Quaneisha. She hated to leave the party, but this was the call she had been waiting on.

Chapter 15

As Kim walked briskly to the park, the sun was starting its descent through the sky. There was a chill in the air, which made Kim shiver, as her skin was still wet from the Jacuzzi. She had no idea why she felt an ominous cloud following her to the park. She had been so worried about Quaneisha, and now she was about to talk to Marissa. But Marissa hadn't given her any indication of what happened, which didn't feel right. Maybe Quaneisha had gotten sick and that's why she hadn't called. Kim quickened her pace.

Climbing the hill toward the park, Kim sent a quick text to Kevin: Meeting Marissa at the park.

As she passed Marissa's house, the van was in the driveway and lights were on in the house. The house didn't look quite right. There was not anything out of place, but the silence felt wrong. Kim shivered, crossed the street, and headed to the park.

Her cell phone rang, and she jumped, taking it out of her pocket to see the display. It was Francis. She frowned.

"Hello," she said.

"Hey, baby. I haven't heard from you. I wanted to tell you the good news," Francis said.

"News?" she repeated.

"I got hired at the plant and I am ready for you to come home. We can be a family again, like we promised your mother."

How dare he bring her mother into this conversation to make Kim feel guilty. She would have been so upset to know what Francis had been up to.

"I don't know if I want to come back," Kim said. "I can't live with the drinking," she replied, shifting impatiently at the corner.

"I am clean and sober, no more drinking for me," her father emphasized each word. "You will come home, no more discussion."

"I have six weeks until the end of summer. At least let me stay until then," Kim pleaded. "That was the agreement."

"I bought your bus ticket already. You leave in one month. I will call you with the details."

"I gotta go."

"Okay, honey. I can't wait to see you. Love you," Francis said, his voice suddenly sugary.

Francis seemed to have erased all his past transgressions with a wave of his hand. Things were supposed to go back to normal, just because he said so. It was not that easy. The distance eased some of Kim's pain but not erased it. He wanted to return her to the role of parent, adult decision-maker, but Kim wasn't ready to try to fill adult shoes again. It felt good to just be a teenager for once. One thing hadn't changed and that was his selfish attitude. He never asked her what she wanted or how she wanted to live. He had no idea how to run a family, yet he was playing the keep-the-family together card.

Kim walked into the park, where she saw Marissa sitting at a picnic table. "Hey, girl, I got here as quickly as possible. I have been so…" Kim stopped talking as she looked at her friend's tear-stained face. "What happened?"

"It has been so f-up these last couple of days," Marissa said. "Q is gone."

"Gone where? Tell me what happened."

"I told her not to trust her father, but she went anyway. I told her to wait on your research, but she went anyway," Marissa whispered through tears.

Kim leaned in to catch what her friend was saying.

"It was a set up from the beginning. The police were watching her father and his crew. Q and her dad's girlfriend went in together. They were searched and arrested," Marissa said. "Our good-for-nothing foster mother refused to go down and see Q until the police insisted she come to a hearing."

Kim's tear-filled eyes were fixed on Marissa.

"We went to the hearing and the judge charged her with a federal crime, and they may try her as an adult. No one stood up for her. She looked so defeated in that courtroom." Marissa threw up her arms. "That B had the nerve to say she got what was coming to her and now she needs to find a replacement so she won't lose any more money. Money is all she cares about. I can't stand her!"

"This can't be happening," Kim replied.

"They appointed a public defender today and continued the indictment over until next week. I have been crying all day. I miss Q so much. I want to help her, but I don't know how."

Kim hugged Marissa and cried along with her friend. Quaneisha was in major trouble and they had no one to help. They were misfits; no one cared what happened to them. They needed someone to care, but Kim didn't know where to turn. There had to be someone to ask, but right now no one came to mind. Adults would judge them falsely as just another group of juvenile delinquents from the streets. But the real criminals were the adults who lied to Q and pulled her into an illegal operation. The adults should pay for the crime, not Quaneisha, who had only trusted her father. Kids are supposed to believe their parents. Putting her trust in her father had cost Quaneisha her freedom; her father had imposed the same lifestyle on his daughter that he chose for himself. Instead of pushing her to have a better life, he selfishly pulled her into the gutter with him.

Kim thought about her father and how he constantly pulled her into the gutter, too. Some parents didn't deserve their kids.

Now Marissa sat broken–hearted, and they both may have lost a friend for life.

Kim felt a resolve start developing in her bones, working its way up to her mouth. "We are going to find a way to help her. I refuse to give up."

"How?" Marissa asked.

"I don't know yet, but I am not giving up," Kim replied.

"I want to believe you, but we are broke," Marissa responded.

"Give me some time," Kim said.

"I'm with you. I want her back. She is the only person in my life who cared about me."

"I care too," Kim replied, hugging her friend again. "I have got to head home."

Marissa stood and they walked in silence from

the park. Kim hugged her again when they reached Marissa's house. "We will find a way."

Marissa nodded, lowering her head as she stepped into the house. She looked so defeated, Kim thought.

Life went from bad to worse in a matter of minutes. Kim didn't know any lawyers, which was exactly what she needed right now. Maybe she could get some free legal help. Someone had to help her. Giving up was not an option. Kim walked onto her street, lost in thought. As she lifted her head, she noticed a police car in front of her house. Fear engulfed her, and she started to jog home. She hoped no one called the police on her. She texted her brother to let him know where she was. Maybe someone was hurt. Kim jogged faster. She could not take any more bad news.

She walked up the driveway heading in the front door, and found the police talking with Kevin's parents. Kevin was sitting in the kitchen, listening.

"Is everyone okay?" Kim asked.

"Yes, the police want to ask you a few questions," Robert said.

"Me? What about?" Kim asked.

"Come sit down. We have assured them that you are in no way mixed up in this drug trafficking."

"What?" Kim asked.

"Do you know Quaneisha?" the police asked.

"Yes, she's my friend and she doesn't do drugs," Kim responded.

"Well, she was arrested for trafficking drugs and your number was in her cell phone. How close are you two?" the policeman questioned.

"She is my friend and only did what her father told her to do. She trusted the adults in her life and they lied to her," Kim replied. "This isn't her fault."

"What do you know about this deal?" they

asked.

"Nothing."

"If you cooperate, it might help her," the policeman said.

"That's all I know. Her father set it all up. Talk to him."

"He is pleading the fifth. Maybe we should take you down to the station," the officer said to frighten her.

Robert interrupted. "She answered your questions and this conversation is over. Anymore and you can speak with our attorney. You can leave now," he said, standing at the front door.

"Fine. But we will be back."

Kim sat there in shock. The police believed the kids had a drug ring, instead of Quaneisha's low life drug-addicted father. They were jamming her up and leaving Quaneisha's father and his friends alone.

Now they had brought trouble to the place she lived. Francis didn't have to worry; her time in California would end soon. No one wanted a kid bringing trouble to their house, and Kim brought the police. Kevin would probably hate her now too. She would go pack her things and call Francis; maybe he could change the ticket.

"Tell us what happened," Allison mother said evenly.

Kim told them how her friend had been duped by her father into bringing him medical marijuana into the prison. She told them how guilty he made his daughter feel for questioning him. Q's father was the real criminal and now he was blaming everything on Q. Kim told them how she hadn't been able to contact Q because she had been on two-weeks restriction. They listened to the whole story.

"We may have a friend who might be able to help," Robert said. "We will have to discuss whether or not you can still see your friends. We will talk more later."

Kim nodded and went to her room. She put on her pajamas and climbed into the bed. She failed her friends and didn't know what to do.

Chapter 16

Kim woke the next morning, mentally exhausted. It took her hours to fall asleep after the police left. She worried about her friend locked away in jail. Francis had placed Kim in dangerous situations, but he had never asked her to do anything illegal. He still had some morals, but Quaneisha's father had none. It had to be horrible to be arrested and face prison, as a result of obeying your parent.

She hoped Kevin's parents could find a lawyer to help her friend. But what if they changed their minds? What if they were upset that the police had paid them a visit? They weren't like Francis, who was always tangling with the police.

While Kim was lying in bed thinking about her worries, Andrea jumped down from the top bunk, changed into her practice uniform, and headed toward the door. Kim watched, wondering if she should try to talk to Andrea about her friend. But Andrea caught Kim's gaze and quickly whipped her head in the opposite direction. The hostility returned ten-fold. The moment at the pool party had only been a small respite from the storm that usually followed Andrea when she was in Kim's presence.

Kim was disappointed, but she didn't have time to worry about this relationship.

Just then, Kim's phone chimed. She grabbed it from the nightstand, and when she heard the voice, she smiled.

"Did you ask Kevin's mom about the lessons?" Davion asked.

"Hold on. Let me ask," Kim said. Then she walked into the hall and knocked on Allison's door.

"Come in," Allison said.

"I forgot to ask you; can I take swim lessons? Davion has offered to teach me."

"Will an adult be there?" Allison asked.

"Kevin's mom wants to know if an adult will be there," Kim said into her phone.

"Yep, my mother will be home. Tell her I'm a certified lifeguard. I've given lessons before," Davion said confidently.

Kim relayed the message and Allison agreed to allow Kim to take the lessons with Davion. Swimming was an excellent skill to have, Allison said, and she insisted on paying Davion a fee to teach Kim.

"Thanks, that's really nice of you," Kim said. She wanted to ask Allison about the lawyer for Quaneisha, but then realized Allison probably hadn't had time to do anything yet. "Yes, you can teach me. She wants to pay you."

"Good, come over in one hour," Davion responded.

Kim showered and grabbed the black one-piece speedo swimsuit Allison bought her at the beginning of the summer and a short white shirt. She was a little nervous about learning to swim. She'd never spent any time in a pool in Texas, and now she was 15, almost too old to learn. She was afraid of looking stupid in front of Davion.

"Good morning," Kim said, as she walked into the kitchen, where Kevin's two brothers sat eating breakfast.

"Hello," they answered in unison, looking up at her and smiling.

Kim liked Kevin's brothers; Julian and Mark; they had been nice since she first arrived. She had focused so much on Andrea and her negativity; she hadn't paid much attention to the boys. The bad overshadowed the good in the family, which was a shame, since there was plenty of good in the house.

"What are you guys doing today?" she asked. She would spend a little more time getting to know the brothers in the family.

"I have an interview for a job this morning," said Mark, the seventeen-year-old whose light brown eyes lit up when he smiled, which was always.

"I have summer school," replied Julian, who was in sixth grade. He looked like Andrea, caramel colored, always moving and laughing. "And then I'm going to camp."

Kim spread peanut butter on her toast. "Okay, have a good day, fellas. I'm headed next door to swim; I mean learn how to swim," she offered.

"Wow, I thought everyone could swim," Julian blurted out.

"Julian, don't say that. It's not polite. He didn't mean anything by it," Mark explained.

"Sorry," Julian said.

"It's okay. We didn't have pools in my old

119

neighborhood, so there was no reason to learn to swim," Kim responded, patting his shoulder. She smiled down at him. "I wasn't offended."

Out front, she could hear Davion's voice talking to Kevin across the driveway. She knew Kevin was upset with her, so trying to get him to understand her side was a waste of time, which hurt. Help was what she needed right now, not anger.

Kevin pivoted toward his sister, anger flashing across his face.

"Trouble just seems to follow you. Now you have involved mom and dad," he said with his back toward Davion.

His words shocked Kim speechless. She had not done anything wrong. Once again, Kevin had formed a judge and jury convicting her and protecting his family. It was obvious now that she was not his immediate concern, but a blemish on his new, perfect family. This was clear evidence that she did not belong in his world. "I have not involved anyone," Kim said.

"Having police at our house is definitely something. You have brought more drama to our house than the rest of us combined. My parents are all that is standing between you and a drunk in a shack."

Davion walked up to where Kevin and Kim were standing and looked at Kim's glassy eyes. "Kevin, that was harsh. Don't condemn her without the facts. It was Kim's friend who made a mistake, not Kim. We all could be in her shoes. Remember when Calvin was arrested for being with someone who committed a crime. We were hanging with the same guys the day before. Have you listened to Kim's side of the story?"

Kim smiled at Davion, grateful that he had come to her rescue.

"Kevin, you know her father bullied her into taking weed into the prison," Kim explained. "And now he is letting her take the fall for it." Confidence returned to her voice. "I have done nothing wrong but try to help a friend. I remember what is like to lose my family and have no one to rely on for help. I will not abandon a friend. It is lonely out here when no one cares." And with that, Kim walked away from her brother and turned toward Davion. "I am ready for my lesson, Davion."

As Kim and Davion walked toward his backyard, Davion said to her, "Kevin is out of line. You did nothing wrong."

"Thanks, my friend is in Juvenile because her father forced her to transport drugs for him. I feel so bad for her. I know what it is like to want your family back together and to feel like you have no one."

Davion lifted her chin. "I understand, too. I miss my dad. I am here to listen if you need me."

Kim nodded.

"And now for your lesson. Put your stuff down on the chair, and we will get started," Davion said. "It'll take your mind off things."

Davion walked Kim into the shallow end of the pool and proceeded to show her how to float and kick her feet using a floatation kick pad, while he held the pad and walked backwards in the water. The water was refreshing and invigorating, and Davion was patient and very knowledgeable about swimming. When he showed Kim how to do the dead man's float, he put his hand gently under her stomach and waited until she felt comfortable before he let go. "Way to go, Kim! You're a natural!" he complimented her.

Kim enjoyed the session. Davion didn't press her for information or condemn her choices in friends. His guidance and touch were confident and gentle. After forty-five minutes, his mother came out of the house.

"Take a break, you guys. I'll make lunch."

Davion and Kim dried off, wrapped towels around their waists and headed to the patio table, where Davion's mother placed their lunch: ham and cheese sandwiches with Doritos and watermelon slices. There were two glasses of sweet iced tea on the table, too.

"Thank you," Kim said, thinking that Davion and his mother were alike. They both made her feel welcome and comfortable.

Davion thanked his mother, as she went back in the house. "You are a quick learner," Davion complimented Kim.

"You make it seem easy," Kim replied as she took a bite of her sandwich. "Thanks again for coming to my rescue with Kevin."

"He will come around. Sometimes friends have to help you see the big picture. I really admire your dedication to your friends," Davion responded.

"They were the only two people to take the time to get to know me when I first came to town. They are real friends and I intend to be a real friend to them. They are good people."

"You are, too."

Kim blushed and looked at her watermelon slice. Davion was giving her a string of compliments and she did not know what to do. He really seemed like a genuine nice guy. She finished her lunch in silence, replaying his kind words.

"I have to get ready for football practice, but I will be around later if you want to go for a run with me or talk. I'll text you when I get back."

"Okay, D, thanks for the lesson. What will you charge me?" Kim asked.

"Nothing. It is something I enjoy doing. We

can meet same time tomorrow."

"Sounds good," Kim replied. She gathered her things and headed for the gate, glancing back at Davion and waving. He was smiling and Kim smiled back. He had been easy to talk to and very supportive; swimming had been great, too. He succeeded in taking her mind off her friend.

Kim sent a quick text to Marissa: Any news?

"I am going to see her tomorrow. Want 2 go?" she texted back.

"Sure, let me clear it with the adults," Kim replied.

That night at dinner, Kim felt invisible. She wanted to reach out to Kevin and his parents for help, but every time she looked at Kevin, she lost her nerve. He'd been so mean earlier in the day when he confronted her about the police visit. He was a stranger sitting across from her, not her brother. His new family was more important to him than the old one. He wasn't treating her like a sister anymore. She was beginning to wonder if she belonged in his new world at all.

She saw so much of herself in Quaneisha. She couldn't abandon her.

"Kim, a few friends from school are coming by tomorrow, and I would like you to meet them," Kevin said.

"Okay," Kim replied, pleasantly surprised. Maybe her brother was seeing the error of his ways. This was a nice gesture. "What time will they come by?" she asked.

"It will be about two. I want you to introduce you to some real people, deserving of your time," Kevin responded.

"What's your criteria for being a real person?" Kim replied, seething, and clenching her fists. "Money?" She could sock him right now. He had totally forgotten where he came from.

Kim stood at the table and glared at Kevin. "I am going for a run. I need some air."

She had every intention of asking Allison if she could go to visit her friend, but now asking seemed impossible. No one had corrected her brother. Kim took that to mean that he was expressing the family's views.

Chapter 17

The next afternoon, Marissa was outside leaning on a car kissing some guy as Kim walked up toward the foster mother's house.

"Hey," Kim called.

"Hey girl," Marissa responded. "This is my boy, Carlos."

"Hello, Carlos," Kim said.

"What's up," he replied.

"Are you still going to visit Q?" Kim asked.

"Yeah, Carlos is taking us," Marissa replied.

"I thought your foster mom was giving us a ride," Kim replied.

"No, she doesn't give a damn about Q. My boy got us though," Marissa responded. "Girl, get in."

Kim stood frozen for a few minutes. Should

she get in the car with a guy she didn't know? He looked like he was a straight-up bad boy, on leave from juvenile. He had multiple tattoos up his arms, and he wore baggy khaki pants, showing his black underwear, white t-shirt with a white bandanna hanging out his back pocket. Kim averted her eyes from Carlos's gangsta apparel. Something was wrong with this picture. "When did you guys start going out?" she asked, stalling for time.

"Two days ago. It was like love at first sight." Marissa kissed him again.

This was crazy. Her friend was all over him and she had just met him. It didn't feel right getting in the car with this guy. He was creepy and the car reeked of marijuana. She had to talk some sense into this girl. "I'll have to get my brother to drop me off. His parents will have a coronary if I go with someone they don't know."

"They won't find out. My baby drives really safe. We will be back before anyone misses you."

"I can't help Q if I am kicked out of the house," Kim replied.

A car honked two short, loud honks. Kim jumped. When she looked up, she saw Davion's adoring brown eyes.

"I saw Kevin and he said you went for a run," Davion said.

"Hey, Davion, this is my friend Marissa and her friend Carlos. Where you headed?" Kim asked.

Davion motioned for Kim to come closer. She ran across the street. "Nowhere, really. Why, you need a lift?"

"Yeah, I was headed to see Q, but I thought her foster mom was driving. Not him," Kim responded.

"I'll take you," Davion said. "We'll follow you," he indicated to Marissa and Carlos.

Relieved to be with a familiar person, someone she knew she could trust, Kim got in the car. "Thanks, I really just want to see my friend."

"Yeah, Kevin's parents would go ballistic if you were in the car with that gang banger," Davion laughed.

"What, he's in a gang for real?" Kim asked.

She'd heard of gangs on television, but she'd never seen a real, live gang member.

"That's what the white rag hanging out of his pocket means. Your friend needs to leave him alone."

Kim nodded. Marissa was hanging with a known gang banger and probably headed for trouble. This was not good. This fling would have to end. One friend in trouble was hard enough.

Frowning, Kim looked back at Marissa and Carlos again, wondering if Marissa knew she was falling into a pit of snakes, ready to bite at any moment.

"I was hoping you were coming by today for a lesson," Davion said.

"I planned to, but I wanted to see my friend Q first. She needs someone. No one is fighting for her, and the police don't care."

"Are you sure she deserves the attention you are giving her?" Davion asked.

"When your parents aren't there to fight for you, you should have someone in your corner. Plus, she was doing what her father told her to do. She doesn't do drugs," Kim said. "Yes, she deserves my friendship and for someone to care enough to help."

Davion pulled up to the juvenile facility on Meadow Lark Drive. The beige, brick building looked like a small prison, with a tall black fence enclosing the rear and side of the building. Marissa had jumped out of the car and her bad boy was peeling rubber down the street. Davion parked.

"I'll wait here," Davion replied.

Kim and Marissa walked up the sidewalk heading toward the main entrance. When they arrived, Kim looked around the lobby. A woman and child were exiting the building; she had a tight hold on his upper arm. The walls were beige stone, the room felt cold and uninviting. A few adults waited in the grey chairs facing the locked door. In the center of the room there an enclosed section with a double thick glass window and a female sheriff sat behind the desk. The sheriff was on the phone.

She pushed a button and spoke into the mike. "May I help you?"

"We are here to see my sister," Marissa announced.

"Parents are the only ones allowed to visit," the sheriff responded.

"I am her only relative. Our foster mother sent me. I need to see her," Marissa insisted.

"Your foster mom will have to come. No kids allowed except inmates."

"Excuse me," Kim chimed in. "Can she have mail?"

"Yes, she can receive mail," the jailor said, pointing to the address on a flyer. "It has to be mailed."

"We drove down here to see her. I need to see that she is alright," Marissa said.

"Leave now before you get an invitation to stay in our facilities," the sheriff said.

"Let's go," Kim replied. She grabbed her friend's arm and pulled her away as the officer clinked the microphone off, then answered the ringing phone. "If we get in trouble, we can't help Q."

"That lady was such a bitch," Marissa spat.

"I wish we could have seen Q, too" Kim

replied. "But we'll have to find another way. Come on. Davion is parked over here."

"Carlos is coming back for me. I'll text him," Marissa responded.

"Marissa, how do you know him?" Kim asked.

"I met his sexy ass last year in math. He was at the park a few days ago. We've been hanging out since then. He's cool."

"You know he's a gang banger, right? That's asking for trouble."

"Kim, he has an extended family of kids that care for each other and watch out for one another. It's better than I got most days," Marissa replied.

"Gangs are not a group of friends hanging out," Kim blurted out. "Drugs, alcohol, and violence are what you have to look forward to if you hang with him."

"Not Carlos, girl. He's different. His gang is his family. Don't believe what you see on TV."

"Marissa, what if you are wrong? Are you prepared to die or go to jail for Carlos?"

"That's crazy. He would never ask me to do that. You are too dramatic. We are hanging out, having fun, end of story. Concentrate on getting Q out. I've got my thing handled."

Kim was speechless. But she didn't really know Carlos; she was judging him based on his appearance and stereotypes. Maybe Marissa was right.

"We'll talk later," Marissa said, as she slipped into the front seat of Carlos's car, which peeled away, dust flying.

"Wait!" Kim yelled.

Marissa waved as she and Carlos disappeared down the street.

"I've got a bad feeling about him," Kim said to herself.

She headed across the street to Davion. "Parent visitors only."

"Wow, sorry," Davion said. "What will you do now?"

"I got the address, so I could send her a letter," Kim replied. "I tried to get Marissa to ride with us, but she's all about Carlos right now."

"He is bad news, Kim. I'm telling you, he stayed in trouble all last year. He even got expelled for bringing a knife to school. Your friend is making a big mistake," Davion said.

"She really misses Q," Kim said. "She's reaching out for somebody."

"I hope she lives to regret her choice," Davion said as they headed back home.

Chapter 18

The house was dark and quiet; Kim took her water to the family room and sat down at the computer. Maybe if she found something to read online, she could salvage the rest of her night. She opened the Yahoo search engine to read the front-page articles, when something caught her eye. Three thousand kids and parents attended the yearly tour of Kearny Mesa's Juvenile Facility... the article began.

As Kim clicked on the pictures of the bathroom and the rooms, her mouth fell open. In the bathroom, metal toilets lined the walls, with no doors for privacy. And the bedrooms consisted of a metal bunk bed with thin mattresses, surrounded by brick walls painted beige. Kim released her breath with a scream, then muffled the noise with both hands covering her mouth.

She opened another picture showing the prison blue t-shirt and orange plastic sandals. How could she leave Quaneisha in such conditions when she wasn't a criminal? She didn't deserve to be locked up.

Kim read on down the page.

The juvenile hall was overcrowded and the kids overflowed into one big room filled with metal bunk beds. Last week a fight had broken out between two female gangs. One girl was interviewed and quoted as saying, "No one should want to be here. Sometimes being in the wrong place at the wrong time can get you caught up in trouble. I just want my little sister to stay away from gangs. Don't be a hard-head like me."

Next, Kim clicked on the link related to gangs, and thousands of articles popped up. The first one she read talked about how kids need companionship and love and they think gangs will provide it. That was her friend Marissa, Kim thought, remembering Carlos. Marissa thought she had lost her best friend and now she was searching for love. She didn't have a family, so she was trying to fill that void with a guy whose family was a gang capable of killing.

Kim knew what it felt like to be without a family. She longed for her family to be whole again after her mother's death. Losing Maggie had been hard, and the hole in Kim's heart was still there. Her mother had always been there for her, sewing clothes, helping with homework, cooking good meals. Luckily, there were no gangs in Kim's Texas hometown. But if there had been, would she have turned to them? The article said gangs are loyal to one another like best friends or family. That sounded good, but they committed crimes, too. Even murder. How could anyone think gangs were positive?

Kim continued reading: turf wars, drugs, and alcohol use were high with gangs.

She began to understand what Davion said. The end of the article said that gang life usually ended in death or jail. Kim was saddened by the violence she saw depicted on the monitor. What had Marissa gotten involved in? Kim shook her head. She hoped Carlos was just a passing piece of dust in the wind, and her friend would have moved on tomorrow.

Kim closed the screen on gang drive-by shootings, and an article about a three-year old who died from a stray bullet. She had to read something uplifting or she would never get any sleep.

She started reading, "If I Were Your Boyfriend" by Earl Sewell. This must be Andrea's book, Kim thought, and she almost put it down; she didn't feel like having a fight. But a chapter drew her in and she read thirty pages before she closed the book and went back to bed.

Kim woke up at nine o'clock the next morning and jumped out of bed. She was already supposed to be at Davion's house for swim lessons. She had not meant to sleep so late, but she must have needed it. Feeling rested and determined, she dressed quickly in her blue one-piece suit, one of only two that she owned. Just as Kim pulled on her grey sweatpants, Andrea stepped into the room.

"He only wants to sleep with you, and then he will throw you out with the trash," Andrea spat.

"What are you talking about?" Kim asked, as she quickly braided her hair into two French braids.

"Your little crush on Davion. Don't get too attached."

"Why do you care?" Kim said with a shrug. "Not that it is any of your business what I do. But—" Kim paused abruptly. "You know, an attitude adjustment might help you get a boyfriend. I don't see Davion or anyone else knocking on the door."

Anger flashed across Andrea's face, and she narrowed her eyes. "If I wanted him, he would be mine."

"Clearly you don't believe that. If it was that simple, he would be inviting you out and we wouldn't be having this conversation. But hey, thanks for the warning." Kim smirked as she walked out of the room.

"Maybe it's Davion that should be warned!" Andrea shouted.

Kim's existence in this house had shifted Andrea's world, and no amount of patience would change that. Kim sighed. "Do what you feel you need to. It doesn't matter to me," Kim said, as she continued walking down the hallway. She was tired of trying with Andrea.

Why was Andrea bringing up Davion anyway, Kim wondered? Offering to help Kim didn't indicate he wanted anything other than a friendship. Davion had never shown any interest in taking it further. Why was Andrea so upset?

"Hey, Kim, I was about to text you," Davion said when she arrived at his house. "I thought you forgot about today."

He ushered her through the house.

"No, I slept a little late, sorry."

"Did you have a hard time sleeping last night?"

"Yeah, but I'm okay," she replied.

"You sure? What's going on?"

"I, um, never mind. We can get started," Kim said, avoiding the question.

"Okay, I thought we would review your first lesson and then I could add a few things to it."

Kim lay down her towel and sweats and

followed Davion down the steps of the pool, noticing his sexy butt, and the way the swim trunks hung on his hips.

"What did you say?"

He smiled. "I said I hope you don't mind getting that hair wet."

"I'm sure I will survive," Kim answered and smiled, thankful she had braided her wild curls. He sure is cute, she thought, especially when he smiled.

"Some women are funny about messing up their hair. I'm just warning you, today it's going to get wet."

Kim laughed as he led her by the hand to the four-foot level in the center of the pool.

"I want you to practice holding your breath under water. Keep your eyes open so I can see them. It is important to see where you're swimming. I will be under there with you."

Kim nodded, not trusting her voice.

She gripped Davion's hand a little tighter, feeling warm all over from the contact. Davion was counting down. Then she felt the pressure of him pulling her under water. Kim felt a little panicked as she closed her eyes tightly and the water finally covered her head. Just in time, she felt the tug back to the surface.

"Great job! Just remember to keep your eyes open next time," Davion said.

They repeated the same drill until being under water with her eyes open felt comfortable to Kim. Davion held her hand with a steady confidence. He would not let her drown.

Now he had her holding the kick pad and kicking her feet with her face in the water. The water felt refreshing, the heated pool was very comfortable to maneuver in, and it helped relax the tension in her shoulders. It didn't hurt that Davion was so patient.

"That's enough for now. Let's get a drink."

Kim followed Davion out of the pool, where he handed her a towel, then dried himself off. They sat at the patio table drinking their sodas.

"You are so easy to talk to, and I really enjoy spending time with you," Davion said, his voice deepening.

"Thanks, but I should be thanking you. You came to my rescue yesterday and my swim lessons are spectacular," Kim said as she stood to leave. "Can I come after dance class tomorrow?"

"Yeah sure, but wait a minute. Can you hang out a while?"

Kim stopped and looked into Davion's eyes. His expression was hopeful and sincere. But why would he want to hang out with her? Kim wondered. He could hang out with anyone he wanted to and he had picked her. No, that was impossible. Andrea must be right. Kim thought about Texas and how the only person she could trust was Keith. He was someone she depended on in tough times, which were often. He was a shoulder to cry on, or an ear to listen, whatever she needed. How do you replace a friend like that? Kim missed him.

Davion stood up and took Kim's hand.

"I was trying to tell you how much I like hanging out with you," he repeated.

"Why?" she asked, startled.

"You're real with me. You're passionate about your friends and what you feel is right. I haven't encountered anyone who put others before herself in a long time. I think that's so cool."

Davion's words shocked Kim into silence.

"I would like to take you to a movie or to lunch, whatever you like. If that's okay?"

"D, did you just ask me out?" she asked.

Kim didn't know what to think. Just this

136

morning Andrea warned her about Davion. Was she right about him wanting sex? Those athletic guys did have reputations with the girls. Look at him, she thought. Who wouldn't want to spend time in his arms? But wait, was he one of those jerks? No, jerks didn't teach you swim lessons, did they?

"Yeah, I just asked you out," he replied smiling.

"Wait, where's your girlfriend?"

"I don't have a girlfriend. I haven't met anyone who interested me before this summer."

"Well," Kim was quick to ask, "Did you ever date Andrea or her friends?"

"No, I try to be polite, but I am not interested in them."

Kim's heart thumped hard in her chest. He looked serious, but this had to be a dream. Then Davion walked closer and pulled Kim's chin up. The wind stilled and the birds stopped chirping. Was he going to kiss her? She could feel his breath on her face. His eyes were a golden brown and his hold was tender and strong.

"Can we go out?" he asked again.

"Yes," she whispered. "I would like to hang out with you."

He released his hold on her chin after her answer, remaining close enough to touch her, though he refrained.

"Good. Tonight?"

Kim gulped hard. "I have to clear it with Allison," she replied. "Could we make it tomorrow night?"

"Sure," he replied.

"Davion, I need your help bringing in the groceries!" his mother yelled.

"Okay, be right there!" Davion yelled back.

"Go help your mom," Kim said. "I have some

things to do at home."

"Let me know what Allison says," he said, reluctant to leave.

"I'll text you later," Kim said, as she grabbed her sweats and headed for the door. When she reached the gate, she looked back at Davion. He smiled and waved.

When Kim walked up the driveway, she noticed Allison's car parked there. She would ask Allison right away. This would be her first real date. What would she wear? Her hair was a mess now. She would need to fix it.

"Hey, Mark," Kim said.

He waved and yelled, "Mom, can you make me a sandwich?"

"I'll do it," Kim responded. This was an opportunity to get to know Mark a little better.

"You go to dance class today?" he asked.

"No, I had a swim lesson," Kim replied. Then she remembered Quaneisha. Oh no, she had been so consumed with Davion, she had forgotten about her friend. Going out with Davion would be fun, but she had to get her friend out of jail.

"No mustard, just mayo," he requested.

Kim nodded her head as she made the sandwich. "Would you like some juice?"

"Yes, please," Mark replied.

Kim placed his lunch on the table.

"Thanks, would you like half?" he asked.

"No, I'll make me one. You enjoy your lunch," Kim encouraged.

"Thanks, Kim," Allison said, as she walked into the kitchen. "I'm late for my hair appointment. See you guys later." She kissed Mark's forehead.

Kim wanted to ask her about the lawyer for Quaneisha, but she was reluctant. When someone offered you help, it was rude to keep asking when it would happen. She didn't want to put pressure on Allison. But they offered to talk to a lawyer, and several days had passed. Meanwhile her friend sat in that cold prison rotting away with gang members who had killed people. She was going to explode if they didn't get help for Quaneisha.

"Kim, honey, come here," Allison said, as she opened the front door. "Our friend, the lawyer, called me back today."

Kim let out a big breath she didn't realize she'd been holding in.

Allison continued. "She said she would come by the house tomorrow to talk to you about your friend."

A tear slipped down Kim's cheek, "Thank you," she replied. It was the only words she could get past her lips. Kevin's parents had kept their word and contacted the lawyer.

"I hope she can help your friend."

"Me too," Kim answered.

Chapter 19

It was almost one and the lawyer would arrive soon. The lawyer had to help her friend; she didn't have anyone else to ask. Kim chose to wear a yellow sundress for her appointment.

Allison had gone shopping with Andrea. She had invited Kim and promised to have her back in time for the meeting, but Kim didn't want to risk being late. Plus, shopping with Andrea did not seem like fun. She had rolled her eyes three times before she left for the mall. It was nice to sit in the room alone and read.

Her phone beeped. "Did you ask the parents?" Davion texted.

Kim had totally forgotten to ask Allison if she could hang out with Davion that night. She didn't want to lie to him, but she couldn't think about anything else until after the lawyer's visit. It was great hanging out with him and she didn't want to miss the opportunity to go out, but Allison was gone, and Robert was at work. She looked at the phone trying to decide what to say.

"I'm meeting with the lawyer to help Q today. Can we go tomorrow?" she texted.

"Cool," he answered.

The doorbell rang.

Kim ran for the front door.

"Hello, I am Amy Joseph. Allison asked me to come by."

Kim was shocked to see a beautiful, caramel-colored woman a few inches taller than Kim looking a lot like Stacey Dash.

"Are you Kim?" she asked.

"Yes, I am," Kim said, beaming. "Thank you for coming. We can talk in here."

"Why don't you start at the beginning and tell me everything," Amy said, as she sat on the couch across from Kim. She took out a notepad and pen.

Kim started talking about how she met her friends in dance class. She told Amy about Quaneisha's first visit to the prison to see her father. She explained how her father told her to bring his medicinal marijuana into the prison. Her friend was doing what her father asked. He knew it was wrong, but Quaneisha didn't.

Amy listened to the whole story and took notes. "This is terrible. First, no parent should ask their child to do anything that is illegal. Your friend will be charged with three to four different crimes. It is a federal crime to transport drugs into a prison. She is being charged with intent to sell and possession of an illegal substance. It can carry up to five years in jail."

"Can you help her, Ms. Joseph? She doesn't deserve to go to jail."

"Oh, call me Amy. And yes, I believe I can help. Can she afford to pay anything?"

"She can't afford it. I could work it off this summer, though," Kim replied.

Amy was silent for a few minutes. "I will make no promises. Let me talk to the DA and your friend. I hate adults who hide behind kids."

"How much will it cost?" Kim asked.

"Well, I usually take a few pro bono cases a year. I can volunteer my time on this one, but I do have a few conditions. First, you cannot volunteer for your friend. If I help her then she will work it off in my office," Amy said. "And if I believe she is guilty, I will not take her case."

Kim smiled. "Thank you so much! Wait until you meet her. You'll see the type of person she is. She was only guilty of putting her trust in her father."

"It makes me angry when I come across situations like this. Drugs and alcohol dependency have separated many families. I know kids hope for unification of their families when they've been separated, but unless their parents take the necessary steps to recover, there is no family," Amy said.

"I hate to see her suffer because of her father's action. I know how parents can disappoint you," Kim replied.

"You are wise beyond your years and a great friend," Amy responded. "Allison and I went to college together. She told me how dedicated you've been to ensuring your friend gets help. I will do my best."

"Her father should have to pay for this," Kim said.

"You are right. I will approach the DA and ask for immunity if she gives up the dealer who gave her the drugs. Also, in order to be charged with possession with the intent to sell, she would have to know it was illegal. Her lack of knowledge could save her from going to jail."

"That's great, how soon could she get out?" Kim asked.

"Slow down, slow down. The system doesn't work that fast. I will have to work on this in my spare time. I promise I will make it a priority, though."

"I was going to write a letter to Q, I mean Quaneisha. Maybe I could tell her about you," Kim said.

"It would be best not to write her. Anything you or she writes could be used against her. Her mail will be read by the officers before she gets it."

"I didn't think of that."

"Who does she live with?" Amy asked.

"She lives around the corner with her foster mom, who doesn't care what happens to Quaneisha," Kim replied.

"I will need to talk to the foster mother since she has custody," Amy responded. "I need to make sure she still has a place to live. If she is released, she will be on probation and one of the conditions of release would be a steady home."

"Will you let me know how things are going?" Kim asked.

"I can't give you specifics about the case because that is a breach of attorney and client privilege. It protects the client. I will let you know if I change my mind about the case. I really hope I can help her."

"Me too," Kim responded.

"I'll let you know my final decision after I get all the facts. Give me a week to gather everything. Here is my card. Call me next Friday to check in," Amy said, as she stood to leave.

Kim closed the door and called Marissa. She was excited to tell her the news. They had help now.

"Marissa, I just finished talking to a lawyer who will represent Q," Kim said.

"Are you serious?" Marissa asked.

"Yes, Q will have to some volunteer work for her services. The lawyer is willing to help her."

"Where did you find her?"

"She is a friend of Allison's. They went to college together. She said she has an angle she may be able to use. I hope it can get her out of jail."

"Yeah, me too," Marissa responded.

"You want to go to the park?" Kim asked.

"No, Carlos is taking me to meet his family. He wants me to be a part of his world. I am really feeling him, Kim."

"Be careful."

"He is not like that. He wouldn't hurt me."

"Gather the facts and ask questions before you get too involved in his world. That's all I'm saying," Kim responded.

"Don't be so paranoid. He's here. Gotta go. I'll text you when I get back."

Something did not feel right about Carlos, and Kim hoped her friend was not digging herself a hole she couldn't get out of. Rescuing friends was becoming hard work.

Kim's phone beeped with another incoming text. For a second, she thought Marissa had listened to some of the things she had told her, but when Kim opened the text it was from Keith.

"Can you talk?"

"Yes," she texted back.

"Hey, I wanted to check in with you."

"Is everything okay?" Kim asked, wondering if Keith had found out anything about her father.

"Yeah, I wanted to get back to you about your father. I really don't have anything to report. I haven't really seen him, which could be a good thing."

"Or it could be a bad thing," Kim added.

"You're right, but let's not speculate one way or the other. I'll keep a lookout for him and let you know when I have something definite," Keith responded.

"Sounds fair," she conceded.

"So, I'll be in touch," he said.

"Thanks, Keith," Kim replied.

He had been her sanity in the middle of the storm her father's drinking had created. The time with him had been wonderful. As she shifted her legs to lean back on her bed, the swimsuit in her hands dropped to the floor, guilt replaced the warm fuzzy feelings. She and Davion were supposed to have their first date the next day. Was she postponing it because deep down she wasn't ready?

Chapter 20

Andrea stomped into the room. "Why do I have to clean up a stupid park!" she huffed, grabbing her sweats out of the drawer.

Kim watched Andrea parade around the room, throwing her pajamas to the floor instead of into her clothes basket, then snatching them up and flinging them in. Kim eased out of the bed and headed to the kitchen to see what had thrown Andrea into such a frenzy.

"Good morning. Today we're helping Mark and his troop do a community clean up," Allison announced. "The Boy Scouts need some extra hands."

"Oh, okay," Kim replied. "Afterwards, can I go out to dinner and maybe a movie tonight with Davion?"

"Sure, Robert and I love his parents and he has been a great friend to Kevin. This will only take a few hours, with all of the extra help," Allison responded.

"Will Julian and Kevin be there?" Kim asked.

"Kevin is at work and Julian will help for a little while, but he has to go to practice. We leave in twenty minutes. Grab a bagel and some cream cheese," Allison replied.

Kim sat at the kitchen table, ate her bagel and drank the orange juice Allison poured for her. This was going to be a long two hours, with Andrea having a fit. Kim finished her breakfast and walked back in the room and to the tornado that was rolling through, leaving destruction wherever it touched. Kim pulled on her sweats, an old faded blue t-shirt, and slipped her feet into her sneakers.

Kim looked down at her shirt. It was one of the last things her father bought her. She touched the shirt and smiled; Francis had always loved her, even with his many faults. He hadn't called lately, which could mean he was up to his old irresponsible self, Kim thought. Or maybe he was working like he had said. It could be either or both. And right now, no news was a good thing. When he started calling again, it would be to give her a date of departure from her new world. She really hoped he was getting his life together; otherwise, she would be returning to hell.

"I still don't think I should have to spend my Saturday doing somebody else's work. The city gets paid to clean up, not me," Andrea complained when the family gathered near the front door.

"We all have a part in our community and it's our responsibility to help keep it clean," Allison informed her.

"Murphy Canyon is not our community, we live in Skyline," Andrea proclaimed.

"Today we are working with several other troops, but we'll be doing a cleanup in Skyline next month. I'll make sure and sign you up to help."

Andrea crossed her arms and turned her head, rolling her eyes.

"Don't roll your eyes at me, little girl," Allison cautioned, placing her hands on her hips. "I'm not the one to be tested."

"Let's go, guys," Robert encouraged as he walked up the hallway.

"I'll follow you, dad," Julian said.

When the family arrived at Murphy Canyon at Hancock Elementary for the cleanup, the Scouts handed out trash bags and divided the volunteers into groups, then showed the groups to the area that needed cleaning. Kim and Julian headed to the field, with Andrea taking up the rear of the line of kids, dragging her feet.

"Here are some gloves to protect your hands," Allison said.

"I'm not wearing those," Andrea replied.

"Start pulling the weeds along the fence," Robert said.

Kim headed to the fence and started picking weeds. Andrea crossed her arms and stared at the working kids.

"Andrea, start picking up the weeds right now," Allison said.

"I can't touch that stuff. It's dirty," Andrea whined.

"Then put on the gloves and start picking up the weeds," Allison insisted.

"Why do I have to help?" Andrea asked.

"You don't have a choice. Open your mouth again and you lose the privilege of leaving the house this week," Allison warned.

"Andrea, here, these bags are already full.

Take them to the truck," Robert said.

"I can't stand her attitude today," Allison admitted.

"She'll come around," Robert replied.

"I hope so," Allison sighed.

Kim watched the exchange between Kevin's parents. Andrea had gotten the easy job transporting the full bags. Her attitude had worked perfectly. Kim thought she was the only one Andrea hated, but it seemed no one was exempt from her negative outbursts. Kim wiped the sweat from her brow and continued picking weeds.

"See, you aren't the only one that Andrea yells at," Julian said to Kim as he reached down and picked up more weeds. "We all deal with it."

Kim never talked to Kevin's brothers about her problems with Andrea.

"We are happy you are here," Mark said. "You're nice and easy to talk to."

"Thanks," Kim replied.

"Thanks for helping," Mark acknowledged.

"Mom, I'm done. That bag broke my nail. This is crazy!" Andrea announced.

"Come here. You have tested my patience today, little girl. You will do as you're told, without complaint. Since you have continued with that nasty attitude, you'll have a one-week punishment of not leaving the house, plus extra chores. Now I don't care if you lose all your nails. Get your butt back over there and help. Now!"

"Robert, your daughter is testing me today," Allison said, walking over to him. "I can't believe that attitude she's developed. We have to nip that right away."

"You're right. I was surprised, too. Tonight, we'll talk to her," Robert promised.

"Mom, I have to leave for work now," Julian

informed Allison. "I'll see you at home later,"

"Thanks, honey," Allison kissed his cheek.

Kim took out her cell phone; she didn't want to make Davion wait any longer for an answer. He should be awake by now. "They said yes, I can go tonight," she texted.

"Great, we can leave at seven," Davion texted back.

Tonight, will be great, Kim thought as she continued picking up the weeds and garbage from the field.

Andrea was still pouting and stomping from the truck to the field with the filled trash bags. She had a wonderful family and didn't know or appreciate it. Her parents were supporting her brother's troop. Kim didn't remember the last time her father attended an event with her. He had never even gone to any of her track meets.

Kevin had great parents who always kept their word. Because of them, Quaneisha had hope with a lawyer. Even when their kids were acting out, Allison and Robert showed their love. Andrea didn't realize it, but she was lucky to have them.

As Kim pulled weeds along the fence, she ended up next to a redheaded girl her age who turned toward Kim and introduced herself.

"Hello, I'm Megan," the redheaded girl said.

"Oh, hi. I'm Kim."

"I'm here with my brother. He goes to Hancock Elementary," Megan said.

"Nice school," Kim replied.

"Are those your parents?" Megan asked.

"No, I'm visiting for the summer," Kim answered. That question hit home for Kim. Feeling suddenly chilled and alone, she shivered.

"Well, this is no way to spend a vacation," Megan said.

"I'm enjoying it," Kim replied. "It's great to clean up the community."

"Yeah, but make sure you see some of the fun stuff," Megan said.

"Okay," Kim smiled, "I'll do that. Where do you go to school?"

"I'm a sophomore at Lincoln Academy. I want to be a doctor," Megan replied. "My number is 858-245-5545; call me so I can plug in your number."

"I want to become a doctor too," Kim responded, as she typed Megan's phone number into the phone.

Attending medical school was a dream Kim thought coming to California would bring her closer to. But she wasn't so sure anymore. She really didn't have any control over her fate.

"Lincoln is a school that has a medical focus for students going into medical careers," Megan said. "I have anatomy and physiology this year."

"That's so cool," Kim replied, excited about meeting another girl who shared her dream.

"We should get together and hang out. I don't know many other girls who want to be doctors," Megan confided.

"Yes, I'll call you." Kim replied.

Kim figured Meagan must have parents like Alison and Robert. Unlike Quaneisha, Marissa, and herself, who had nobody to help them live their dreams. A high school that specialized in medicine would be the perfect school for her, but she'd probably never get there. Kim watched the skinny girl with red curls walk back toward her parents. California could have been a dream come true for Kim, but now she didn't know if she would get to stay here. Plus, she lived with the wicked witch from the west, who didn't want to share her life with Kim. Just then, Andrea walked up to her.

"It is time to go," she said, then turned and walked off.

Kim saw Allison and Robert picking up the tools and the last of the bags and walking toward the parking lot. Kim headed toward the car. "Come on, Mark," she motioned to Kevin's little brother.

Mark ran up next to Kim. "Thanks for helping. I'm glad you live with us."

Kim smiled, "Thank you." His words warmed her heart. As the two of them walked toward the car together, her phone beeped twice.

"Tonight, will be great," Davion texted.

"Yep," she texted back. Then she read the second text.

"Keep in touch," Megan texted.

"I will," Kim responded, as she sat back in her seat in the SUV.

"Thanks for helping clean the community today. It is important to have a part in keeping our environment clean. Now let's go get some lunch," Allison said.

Chapter 21

Kim walked to the closet and pulled out a pair of Hollister jeans shorts and a white sundress and laid them on the bed. She could not decide what to wear for her date. She had just finished her shower after waiting an hour for Andrea to finish her bath. This was her first real date and she wanted to look special. Kim pulled out a fuchsia ribbed top and laid it over the shorts. She decided on the shorts and then put the sundress back in the closet. Kim put lotion on her legs, and then got dressed.

Kim let her sandy ringlets hang down over her shoulders; she glanced in the mirror and applied her lip-gloss. She was ready with thirty minutes to spare and was about to leave her room when her phone rang. An unknown number flashed across her screen. Kim hesitated; she was overdue for a call from her father and she just couldn't have him ruin her first date.

The phone rang again; Kim sighed and answered the phone with a tentative, "Hello."

"Kim, hello," the voice said.

"Hello," Kim answered, trying to recognize the voice. It sounded familiar. But she couldn't quite place it.

"It's Keith. I have worried about you from the last day that I saw you," he replied. "How are you?"

"Keith! Hey! I am fine. I didn't recognize your number. Where are you calling me from?" she asked, her stomach suddenly filled with butterflies.

"Work number. I'm on a break." Keith replied. "Look, you've been on my mind since our last conversation. We talked about your dad, but not you. I felt like you were skimming the surface. Are you really okay? Tell me everything."

"It is so different here. It has its high points and a few low ones," Kim replied. She started from the beginning of the summer and told Keith almost everything, from her new friends to the tension between her and Andrea. She just left out the part about Davion, though she wasn't quite sure why. This was like old times, talking to her friend and confidant.

"Don't give up on Andrea. Some people adjust to change very slowly. Give her time and she will come around," he advised her. "So, tell me, are you happy?"

Kim didn't know what to say at first. She thought about that word and realized it was not quite how she felt. San Diego was more than she could have expected, she had been given so much. Kevin's parents were great; but this life had its own challenges. No, "happy" was not the right word for her feelings. "Keith, I definitely feel grateful and less stressed."

"Sometimes happiness comes in different degrees," Keith replied.

Kim knew Keith was right. She thought back to a time in Texas when she thought food would make her happy. But she had food now. Then she looked at her clothes and remembered thinking new clothes would make her happy. All those things around her had not made her happy. Happiness was too complicated to dissect right now.

"It can get complicated. I was studying philosophy in a four-week summer session class and I've been analyzing everything," Keith said. "I want you to find happiness, Kim. You deserve it."

"Thanks, it's a lot to think about. Tell me about school. Did you love it?'

"I enjoyed it. I can hardly wait for fall term to start. I felt so alive on campus; it has been a dream come true. Just like your dream of moving back to California," Keith replied.

"Yeah, you're right. It's great that you've followed your dreams. Thanks for reminding me of mine," Kim responded.

Talking to Keith brought up a lot of feelings from Kim's past. "I miss our talks," she told him.

"Me too. It's great to know you are okay. There are so many opportunities out there for you to utilize."

"Well, if I stay maybe I'll get the chance, but as it stands, I will leave at the end of summer," she said.

"Your dad should want the best for you. I would love for you to be here, but I recognize the fact that your life would be better there. I can't be selfish, and he shouldn't be either."

"You wish I was there?" Kim asked.

"Well yeah, of course I do. You became a positive part of my life and I enjoyed the time we spent together."

"That is the sweetest thing I have ever heard," she responded. "Have you seen my father?"

"I passed him yesterday walking down the street toward your house," he answered.

"Did he look sober? He told me he stopped drinking."

"That I don't know, but I'll find out. You can't come back to that."

"Exactly, but I may not have a choice," she admitted. Kim looked at her watch. Forty minutes had flown by while she talked to Keith. He had always been easy to talk to and look at—so tall and handsome. Confident, but not conceited. It was flattering to know he missed talking to her. He had been a light in the dark tunnel of her life. She wished she could see him again. But she was late.

"Hey. Keith, I've gotta go. I was headed out with a friend when you called, but I lost track of time catching up with you."

"No sweat. I'll give you a call later, okay?"

"Yep, call me back as soon as you know something. Talking to you always makes me feel better."

"Alright, Kim. Later."

"Later, Keith."

And with that Kim rushed out of her room, heading toward the front door, where she saw Davion talking to Julian and Mark in the family room. "Hey," Kim said.

"Hey, Kim. I'm just down here talking to the fellas. Are you ready?" Davion asked.

"Yeah, sorry I am little late," Kim replied.

"No worries. I just got here," he said.

The front door opened, and Allison and

Andrea walked in. When Andrea saw Davion in the family room, she stopped midsentence to smile and wave at him.

"Allison, we are leaving now," Kim responded, making sure Andrea was watching.

Andrea looked from Kim to Davion and back to her mother, who was grinning.

"You have got to be kidding me," Andrea snapped. They are going out?"

Andrea rolled her eyes at Kim, and then stomped off to her room.

"Don't worry about her," Allison said, as she watched her daughter exit the room. "Have fun and be safe."

Kim walked out the door, wondering what had set Andrea off this time. She hoped Keith was right. and time would change Andrea's attitude, because it only seemed to be getting worse.

"What was her problem?" Davion asked.

"I don't know. I seem to bring out the beast in her."

They both laughed as they got in his car.

"Where are we going?" she asked, determined to not let Andrea ruin her evening.

"How about a movie?" Davion asked.

"Sounds great," she replied. Kim looked over at Davion with his white Nike t-shirt that said, 'Quitting is not in my vocabulary,' and smiled. The words seemed to fit his profile. The blue basketball shorts hung perfectly on his narrow waistline. "What shall we see?"

"What kind of movies do you like?" he asked.

"I like action movies or funny movies, but I'm open," she replied.

"Do you want to see the new Fast and Furious movie? I think they're on the fifth one."

"That's fine," Kim answered.

157

Davion looked over at Kim and smiled, "You look great tonight. I'm happy you agreed to go out with me."

"You are teaching me how to swim. If I said 'no,' I might find myself drowning at our next session," she teased.

"Are you trying to bribe me into taking it easy on you?" he asked.

"Well…" she answered, laughing.

"Forget it, you get extra laps tomorrow."

They both laughed.

"You are so easy to talk to, Kim," Davion admitted.

"You make it easy," she replied.

"I thought we would go to Fashion Valley to the theatre," Davion told her, as he turned left.

"I haven't been there yet," Kim said. So far, she had only been to Plaza Bonita, right near the house. But once they arrived, she could see that Fashion Valley was different than the malls she was used to. Nordstrom was on one end and Michael Kors and Louis Vuitton was in the middle. "Wow, I've only seen these stores on television," Kim exclaimed.

"I rarely shop here, but they have great restaurants and I like the theatre."

"Two tickets for the new Will Smith movie please," Davion requested. The attendant handed him the tickets and they began walking toward the entrance, when they heard a loud girl yelling at the attendant. They both turned.

"I want my damn money back, that movie was whack," the girl in the pink-and-yellow pajamas yelled. "Someone better help me up in this bitch, before I get louder." The attendant was speaking with the manager, and the line was getting longer, so they gave her a complimentary ticket for her next movie. She started to walk off, smiling at her victory, when she noticed Kim and Davion. "Davion, hey baby, I haven't seen you in a while."

Davion looked shocked at her words. "Let's go on in, Kim."

"Wait, did you just ignore me?" the girl yelled.

"I'm sorry. Do I know you?" Davion asked.

"I'm Deja, the girl who sat behind you in Algebra II last year. I know you remember me. I'm the fine one who had the red braids. I gave you my number and you never called. What up with that?"

"I'm in a relationship. As you can see, my girl and I are late for our movie," Davion answered.

"You don't know what you are missing," she replied, as she pulled her dingy pink pajama top down over her belly fat to expose her cleavage.

Kim watched the exchange, holding back her laughter.

"Admirer?"

"More like a scary stalker. Who does that?" he asked, as they walked into their theatre. "I am happy she wasn't coming to this movie."

"Me too," Kim replied.

"You have me all to yourself," he said as he moved the cup holder so that he could hold Kim's hand.

Kim smiled and turned to watch the movie. She could hardly believe her luck. She was out on a date with Mr. Gorgeous, and he proudly said they were in a relationship. Wait, who did he mean? "Davion, what did you mean out there, with the relationship thing?"

"Oh, I was hoping it would be you. I know it's early, but I'm willing to take it at whatever level you want," he replied.

The movie started with a huge explosion, and Kim snuggled closer to Davion, enjoying the security she felt with him. She remembered the last time she snuggled into someone, when she and Keith kissed on her couch, and how good that felt. How could she forget him so easily?

She had too much going on for a relationship. She was trying to save her friend. She struggled to get along with Andrea.   Plus, who knew where she would end up at the end of the summer? It would not be fair to Davion to start something she could not continue. She looked over at him. He smiled. She gave him a tentative, guilty smile.

"No pressure," he whispered in her ear.

Kim nodded. It was hard to deny that she was beginning to like Davion more than just a friend. He was easy to be around and talk to, and he was more than cute. He seemed to understand her. He never questioned her devotion to her friends. And he knew what it felt like to lose a parent. But she didn't have an answer for him just yet. She felt confused after talking to Keith.

"Give me some time," she whispered back.

Davion nodded his head.

They watched the rest of the movie in silence, holding hands.

Chapter 22

It had been a wonderful evening the previous night with Davion. First, they went to a movie and afterwards they sat in the car and talked. Today, she would have her third swim lesson, which Kim was looking forward to. Davion was a gentleman; she felt tingles in her—stomach just thinking about the way he smiled.

"Move your shoes out of my way!" Andrea yelled, bringing Kim out of her dream world.

"I was just about to put them on," Kim responded.

"I don't care what you are doing. Move them! You are not special. And you won't keep Davion's attention," Andrea spit out.

"Yeah, okay. Whatever," Kim responded.

As she watched Andrea stomp out of the room, dripping with attitude, Kim put on her tennis shoes and grabbed her phone. There was a missed call from Marissa at midnight. She would call her back after the swim lesson. She hoped everything was all right with her friend; she hadn't called since they spoke at the park.

Kim took out Amy Joseph's card and called her office. Maybe that's what Marissa had questions about. It had been a while since Kim and the lawyer spoke.

"May I speak to Mrs. Joseph?" Kim said into the phone.

"This is Amy. Hello, Kim, how can I help you?"

"Hello, Amy, I was calling to see if I could get an update from you about my friend Quaneisha," Kim said.

"Well Quaneisha did give me permission to talk to you. She has a decision to make: the DA is willing to drop the charges if she names the dealer who gave her the drugs and implicates her father. She will have to be on probation, but she can get out of jail immediately, and have a normal life."

"That's great! Did she give you the names?" Kim asked.

"No, she didn't want to implicate her father. He had no problem putting her in danger, but she doesn't want to hurt him. I realize it is hard to think about getting your parents in trouble, but your friend has to think about her future."

"Can she just give the information on the dealer?"

"The DA wants both of the parties involved. Her father is already serving time. He will get a little more added to it. But if she doesn't provide the information, she could ruin her life before it starts. It is hard to get back the time she misses if she goes to jail," Amy said.

"So, she has to tell you the names or she goes to jail?" Kim asked.

"Yes, that is the deal," Amy answered.

"How long does she have to make a deal?"

"She has two days to decide. If you want to say anything to her to help, I am willing to give her a message."

"Tell her sometimes kids have to make decisions that are hard because our parents aren't capable of making them. I had to choose what was best for me and leave my father, and I think if my father wasn't sick, he would agree with my decision. She has to tell the truth, so she can have a future. No one should be mad if she tells the truth."

"Thanks, Kim, I will tell her. You are wise beyond your years. I will let you know what happens," Amy responded, as she hung up the phone.

This was awful. Kim understood Quaneisha's reluctance to turn her father in. Could Kim give up information on Francis? He loved her and she hoped he wouldn't ask her to do anything illegal, but if he did, could she really watch him go to jail? She still loved him despite his problems.

Kim grabbed a piece of toast and headed toward the door.

"Hey, what's wrong with you?" Kevin asked.

"Oh, hi, Kevin. Q has to turn her father in to be able to get the charges against her dropped. I am just worried about her. Who wants to turn in their own father?"

"Obviously she should. He sounds like a lowlife just like Francis, and you know I would turn him in without a second thought. This is a no brainer. If she can't see that, then you need to drop her. You have done enough to help her," Kevin responded.

Kim walked out the door toward Davion's

163

house for her lesson. Her brother didn't understand her dilemma. He only saw things two ways: right or wrong, no gray area. He had forgotten all the good times the family had before Maggie died.

"Hey, Kim, I had a great time last night and…" Davion voice trailed off. "What's wrong?"

"I just spoke with Q's lawyer."

"Okay."

"Q can beat the charges if she turns in her father and the dealer."

"Wow, how do you turn in your parents?"

"Exactly. Even bad ones are loved," Kim responded.

"Yeah, but she has to know he put her in that predicament, so he has to take the responsibility as the adult," Davion responded.

"Yeah, I know. I hope she sees it that way."

Davion hugged her. "You are a great friend and Q is lucky to have you."

"Thanks," Kim said, giving him a small smile. It was comforting to have someone to talk to who didn't condemn her actions. It felt good being held.

"You have done all you can do for her, and now it is time for her to make a choice for her own future," Davion said.

"You are right," Kim said. "Thanks. Now I am ready for my lesson."

Kevin said the same things, but it sounded better coming from Davion. They were both right. She had done all she could do for her friend, and now Q had to make her own decision.

Davion released Kim from the hug and led her to the pool.

"Today you learn how to tread water. First, sit down on the edge." He took her legs and mimicked the movement he wanted her to produce under water. "People call it riding bicycles, but I find it helps to show your legs what to do, also."

"Like this," Kim responded.

"Perfect," Davion answered. "By the way, did you enjoy our date?'

"Yes, it was fun."

"I was hoping you would go out tomorrow with me."

"Sure, what do you want to do?" she answered reluctantly.

He sure means business, Kim thought. But she had no business starting something with somebody as nice as Davion when she probably wouldn't be in town much longer.

"My mom's making lunch for us to take to the beach," he answered.

"Wow, you have this all figured out," she said.

"I'm a planner, and I can always hope for the best."

They continued with the swim lesson, going over her strokes and doggie paddle that he showed her the day before. Kim swam a few laps forward and then backwards.

"You're doing great. Just be sure you always take a breath with every other stroke. I noticed that sometimes you forget. Next time, we'll jump in the deep end. That is enough for today," Davion announced.

Kim followed him to the patio. She had found someone special.

"I am going for a run later today. Wanna come with me?" he asked.

"Rain check? I have dance class this afternoon."

"Count on it. And remember, don't beat yourself up about other people's bad decisions," he said.

"I'll remember. Thanks again."

Kim waved as she headed home to change for dance practice. She had given Quaneisha all the help she could give her, and now she had to make her own choices. No amount of worrying in the world could change things for her friend. Kim had to let go and hope for the best. She thought about calling Marissa but decided she would talk to her at practice. Back at home, she quickly showered off the chlorine and changed for dance class.

As she approached the class, Kim thought how odd practice would be without Quaneisha there, but at least Marissa would be there to talk to. Kim headed to the park at a slow jog. The class was stretching when she arrived. She looked around, but Marissa was missing.

She took out her phone and texted her. "At practice. You coming?"

"Not today. With Carlos," Marissa answered.

Kim dialed the number. "Marissa you got to come. I have news about Q."

"I have other plans. What about Q? Just tell me," she answered.

"She can get out if she talks," Kim responded.

"She ain't doing that. Family comes first," Marissa responded.

She was shocked by Marissa's attitude; she seemed different and Kim had a feeling Carlos was behind her new changes. Some changes weren't good ones.

"Wrong is wrong and her father shouldn't want her to do time for his actions," Kim said. "Anyway, I hope she decides to tell the truth."

"Marissa, get off the fuckin' phone!" Carlos yelled in the background.

"I gotta go. I'll talk to you later."

"Wait, why did you call last night?" Kim asked, as the phone went dead.

166

Chapter 23

Andrea was at the movies with her friends, so Kim had the room to herself. It was hard to clear the buzzing in her head after all the activity of the past few days. She pulled the covers up to her neck and snuggled into her pillow, grabbing her Harry Potter book to read. It had been a few weeks since she last read it and she was anxious to get lost in the adventure of Hogwarts.

No sooner than she opened her book, Kim's phone started ringing

"Hey Kim, it's Keith. I saw your father." Kim sat up a little straighter. Keith had her full attention. Finally, the information she needed to help her learn if her father was telling the truth or not.

"Remember Sistah Gal, the one from the house down the street where the winos hangout?"

"Yeah," Kim answered.

"Well, she's been staying with your dad. I saw them leaving your house. I've not seen him drinking, but he's still hanging out where the other drunks hang out. All I can say is that if you are sober, you don't hang out with drunks. I am sorry, but he's not acting sober."

"Thanks, Keith. I'm not surprised, but I'm a little disappointed," Kim revealed.

"I hate to be the one bringing bad news, but I don't want to lie to you."

"It is one of the reasons I respect you. Don't worry, it's okay. I'd rather have the truth," Kim replied.

"I wish I had better news for you. How are things on your end? How are Kevin's parents treating you out there?"

"Kevin's parents are cool," Kim said.

"Go on."

Kim wanted to say more, but she really hadn't given her place in the family much thought. She'd been fighting so hard for her friends that her own needs had become unimportant. Kevin's parents provided for her just like their other children, but she didn't feel like part of the family. She felt more like a visitor and everyone treated visitors well, right? She didn't know where she fit in.

Kevin had changed since he came to live with them, and she was confused about their relationship. She always considered him her brother, and she still did, but she wasn't sure how Kevin felt now that he was living well with his real parents. Maybe that was it—Allison and Robert weren't her parents. That must be why she still felt like a guest. Finally, she told Keith, "I am a visitor here, but I am treated well. To be honest, I don't really know where I fit in."

"Have you talked to Kevin?" Keith asked.

"Funny that you say that. Sometimes I feel like it's me against the world. Kevin doesn't seem to understand me anymore."

"We all change as we mature and grow up, but sometimes we need to be reminded of what's really important. Don't give up on him. You need to talk to him and tell him how you're feeling. You're dealing with a lot, and he could help if you let him."

"You're right," Kim said. "I should try talking to him."

She wondered if Kevin could really listen to her. He seemed more selfish than she remembered. He only seemed to care about his new family and preventing anything from disrupting his new world.

"Maybe he's a little unsure of his place, too," Keith continued. "He might be scared he could lose it all, and then where would he go? Sometimes we only see our point of view, but there is always another side to the story. Ask him how he feels."

What Keith said made sense. She hadn't thought about what Kevin might be feeling.

"Thanks. I never thought of it that way. I'll talk to him," Kim said.

"Oh, and Kim?"

"Yeah?"

"Do me a favor and have some fun," Keith advised.

Had she been having any fun? she wondered. Well, she took her first dance class; which is where she met Quaneisha and Marissa—that was fun. She'd met Davion and gone out on a date—that was fun too. Things weren't all bad. Despite the drama from her friends and Andrea, and not knowing where she fit in, she was having more fun than she realized.

"I will," she said.

"Kevin's family sounds like it is worth working through the kinks. Don't come back here to the nightmare you were living."

"Yeah, maybe you are right." Kim said, but she wished staying was that easy. She wanted more than to be treated well; she wanted to be accepted. Not to mention, it was hard coming from a family that loved her. In the end, she was not tied to Kevin's family by the bonds of blood or love. "You make it sound so simple."

"I know it's not, but promise me you will work on doing your part?"

"I promise," she whispered.

"Okay, I gotta go. I'll call you in a few days."

Kevin was her brother and it would only be fair to talk to him. Kim made a mistake before when he ran away, ignoring his feelings. Kevin kept telling her how he felt about their father and his poor behavior, but Kim only argued with him. Maybe she would understand Kevin better if they talked. He had to love her to bring her here, right? This was his family and he was the one who knew how they worked. She would talk to him tomorrow.

She opened her book and held it, but she couldn't read. What was her father doing with that girl? She was a hundred years younger than him, after all he was fifty-five. This was so embarrassing. He could be her father. Francis could go to jail if he continued that behavior. She had to set him straight. Adults didn't act like that. This would ruin his reputation for life. Once again, he was acting like the teenager, and she felt like the adult. He had to still be drinking. That was the only explanation for his behavior.

How in the world did he expect her to come back to that crap? Life was different for her now. Just the thought of her old life made the pressure in her chest build and sweat drip down her forehead. This had to be how heart attacks felt.

It had been a while since Kim thought about the many nights she had no food and her father didn't come home. She had been alone in the dark because he didn't pay the bills. Not to mention the days she had to boil the water they collected from their neighbor, Tim, in order to bathe. It had been so hard to live with her father, the drunk. If he was still drinking, then she would be in the middle of hell with no way out.

She tried once again to read her book, but it was too hard to block out the pain and disappointment. She wanted Francis sober and well, but she couldn't fix him. She thought it would be easier without her to start over and get himself together, but it looked like nothing at all had changed.

Kim's phone rang again breaking her sober mood. "Hello?" she answered.

"Baby girl!" her father yelled.

"Dad?"

"Yep, it's me. I was telling your friend, that cop, that you were coming home soon."

Tears fell down her cheeks. He wanted to drag her back to that hell. How could any parent want that for their child?

"Baby, you hear me? It's time to come home. I let you spend the summer there. Now it is time to get back here and start school," her father insisted. "Daddy misses you. I miss your smile and the way you got so excited when you were doing your cheerleader dances. The house is so lonely without you. I can't stand the quiet empty rooms any longer. Baby, come home."

"Dad, I can't live like that anymore. It's not fair to me. How can you expect me to live like that?" Kim asked.

"I have fixed things. It will be just like when your mom was here," he replied.

"You paid all the bills?"

"Well, yeah," he answered.

"Then why are you calling me on Tim's phone?" she asked.

"They gave our number away. I am getting one of those cell phones. No one really has home phones anymore. I've been working hard to build a place for you."

"Why do you have that girl at our house?" Kim asked.

"What girl are you talking about? I have a new woman in my life. She has had a hard time, but she is a sweet lady."

"What sweet lady? The hookers from down the street. What is she, 16 or 17?" Kim asked question after question.

"No, she was forced into that life by her mother. She is such a sweet person. You guys are going to be great friends. Give it a chance. She has been helping me clean the house for you."

"Keep that tramp away from my things. I don't want to be friends with her. What I need to know is when you had your last drink," Kim demanded.

"I have my drinking under control. I'm working regularly now, and I only have a beer on weekends. Most men have a drink on weekends. It's nothing like before, honey. I've got it together now. Don't worry. I'm better."

You shouldn't be drinking at all, Kim wanted to tell her father, but she knew it was no use.

"Dad, I've gotta go. I'm tired," she said, trying to keep her voice from cracking.

"Okay, but you have two more weeks, then you're coming home."

"Bye, Dad."

Kim closed her book. If her father was

hanging out with other drunks, he was most likely still drinking. He could not hold onto a job when he started drinking, and then he didn't eat or sleep until he blacked out. Kim could see the piles of empty bottles and trash littering his bedroom.

She wiped the tears that kept falling down her cheeks. Why was life so hard, she wondered? She wanted to go talk to Kevin, but he was the wrong person to talk to. Maybe it was easier for Kevin to hate Francis because he knew who his real father was. The trouble for Kim was, Francis was her legal father and she would have to obey him. The thought of it made her head spin, and she felt lightheaded and dizzy.

Chapter 24

Kim tossed and turned all night trying to clear her head. After giving up on sleep, she pulled back the covers, and grabbed her clothes to take a bath. Her thoughts were jumbled and confused. Her father was demanding her compliance. As her legal parent, he deserved her obedience, but it was unfair to ask her to return to the hell she left in Texas. Kevin and his siblings were lucky, she thought as she soaked in the bathtub. They got to be kids and think about kid things, not the kind of adult problems Kim was forced to think about. And they knew they would always be provided for, not only with material possessions, but with love and understanding.

How different their life was from Kim's when she lived in Texas. She still remembered the days she brought food home from school, so she could have dinner. The school's breakfast program satisfied her hunger on many days.

Kim let the hot water relax some of the tension in her back. She would have to reason with her father, she figured. There was no way she could return to her old life.

Kim wrapped her fluffy towel around her body, allowing the warmth to comfort her, as she began to dry off her body. She thought about Quaneisha and Marissa. She was not the only one suffering right now. Neither one of them had parents who cared enough to be responsible for them. Everyone needed someone on their side. And she was on theirs.

Kim grabbed her phone off the sink and dialed Marissa. It was early, but she should still pick up the phone. The phone went to voice mail. Kim was starting to get worried; Marissa hadn't called in days. Kim made a mental note to call again later.

Since another swim lesson was scheduled for later, she dressed in some jean shorts over her blue one-piece swimsuit and went to the kitchen to eat. There was an abundance of food, and all the kids took it for granted because it was always available. They were lucky to not have to experience hunger pain.

She ate a piece of toast and a bowl of cereal. The house was starting to wake up with activity, but Kim felt like escaping the jolly atmosphere. She wanted to talk to Kevin, but it just didn't seem right to burden him with her problems. He finally had a chance to enjoy being a young adult, and she didn't want to rain on his parade.

"Your phone is ringing," Julian said, as he walked around the corner from his bedroom.

"Thanks," Kim answered, hoping it was not her father again. She was not ready to tackle that bridge right then. She quickened her pace. Maybe it was Marissa or the lawyer with information about Quaneisha. She picked up the phone, and just missed the call. She hit the "Call Back" button.

"Hey, you called?" Kim asked.

"I know it is a little early, but I need to cancel our session today," Davion said. "I have to run a few errands for my mom, but I would like for you to come along."

"When are you leaving?" Kim asked

"In thirty minutes," he replied.

"Hold a second, let me check," Kim said, as she laid the phone down and knocked on Allison door to ask permission. Relieved that Allison had said she could go, Kim returned to her phone.

"Yes, I can go. Let me change, and I will be right over."

This would be great. She needed some time outside to think things through. She removed the swimsuit and picked a red tank top with her jean shorts. She grabbed her phone and flip-flops, and headed out the door, waving to Kevin's brother Mark as she closed the front door.

"Thanks for coming. My mom has a baking business, and sometimes I make deliveries. We have five cakes to deliver to three stops. It would have been a long ride by myself. I hope you aren't disappointed about the lesson."

"No, it's fine. I've got a lot on my plate, and it'll be a nice distraction," Kim said.

"Are you still worried about Q?" he asked.

"Yeah, and Marissa too. She's hanging with the wrong crowd. Plus, I have other things going on too," Kim replied. She frowned and turned her head toward the passing landscape.

"What's going on?" Davion asked. "You can talk to me."

"It's just...never mind," Kim replied.

"Hey, I'm a good listener. Ask my mother. She will tell you I'm great at everything," Davion smirked.

Kim smiled. "Your mother is your reference?"

"Well, yes. You gotta utilize your resources," he said with a grin. "Who knows me better than my mother?"

"You're too funny. I don't know where to start. Let's see. My dad wants me to come back to Texas in two weeks," Kim blurted out.

"Wow, is it a good thing?" he asked. "I mean I would like to see you stay, but what do you want?"

"You don't understand. It doesn't matter what I want. My father gets to make the decision. It has been like a fantasy to come here and spend the summer. When I lost my mother, my world changed forever," Kim informed him. "It affected all of us, especially my father. He started drinking a lot. Eventually, the only thing that mattered was his next drink."

"Is he still drinking?"

"He says it is only on the weekend, but some friends from home have reported bizarre behavior, and he's dating a really young woman. I think he is still doing the same thing."

"That's all bad. My uncle is an alcoholic, and he is doing some time for vehicular manslaughter right now. That's a hard choice."

"Tell me about it. I still love him, even though his actions have caused me a great deal of pain. I don't want to go back to that turmoil, but I don't seem to have a choice," Kim responded.

"Hold that thought, let me deliver this cake."

"You shouldn't have to return to an unsafe environment," Davion told Kim as soon as he got back into the car. "No court would force you to return," Davion replied.

"Are you saying I should get a lawyer and take him to court?" Kim asked.

"If necessary. A lawyer would look out for your best interest. Your dad's not doing that."

Kim sighed. "I don't know. I don't think I could stand taking my own father to court. I don't want to hurt him. There has to be another way."

"Maybe it won't come to that. Have you talked to Kevin or his parents?"

"No, Kevin is still adjusting to his new transition. I don't want to add to his tension, and those are his parents. I really don't want to be a problem," Kim answered. "Andrea made it perfectly clear that I am the outsider who doesn't fit into their family. I don't want to live with someone with whom I'm constantly bickering."

"Allison is a very kind person. She introduced you to the lawyer that helped Q. I bet she can help you too. You should talk to her."

"Really?"

"I find adults can sometimes be helpful. Especially, with the important stuff. Give it a try. What can it hurt?"

Kim remained silent.

"Plus, she seems really cool," Davion added. "I bet she will surprise you."

"Adults have been disappointing in my life so far," Kim remarked.

"What about Kevin's parents?" he asked.

"Not yet, but I find it hard to trust easily," Kim said.

"All adults aren't bad. Don't let a rotten apple spoil your views, my Granny always says," Davion replied.

"Maybe you're right. I'll run it by Allison when she gets home tonight."

"That's more like it," Davion said as they pulled into another driveway. "This is our second stop. The last one is out in La Jolla."

Kim felt a weight shift off her chest. Maybe Allison could offer her a few suggestions. Allison was easy to approach.

When Davion returned to the car, Kim said, "I get so tired sometimes of wanting the adults in my life to do what's right."

"Yeah, I hear you. My mom says she lost the manual that came with me, so she has to wing it. I will not excuse your father's behavior, but maybe he is doing the best he can," Davion agreed with Kim.

"I am just so tired of all of this. It was hard to sleep last night. Then I woke up exhausted. I feel like my body aches all over".

"Maybe you should see a doctor. Sometimes stress in your life manifests itself in your body," Davion suggested.

"A doctor is a luxury that I don't have. I'm sure I'll feel better once this issue is resolved," Kim assured him, as she started coughing and struggling to catch her breath between coughs. "Water please," she mumbled.

Davion pulled off the highway into a gas station, and quickly purchased her a bottle of water. "Drink slowly," he cautioned.

"Thanks, that was so weird," she said, as she wiped her mouth with the tissue he passed over. "I feel a little better," she said, stretching the truth. The truth was she felt a little worse, even though the coughing stopped. She looked over at Davion and smiled, trying to alleviate the worry lines etched on his face. "Let's get to the next stop. I'm getting hungry."

"We aren't too far, and then we will stop for lunch," he responded.

Kim settled back in her seat and briefly closed her eyes. She felt tired and wanted to take a nap. Her eyes didn't seem to be working right. Everything looked blurred. But she could not be sick. Her father couldn't afford health insurance, and she didn't want to burden Kevin's parents. Her symptoms would pass, she hoped. Meanwhile, she had more important things to worry about. Then her phone rang.

"Hello, Kim, this is Amy. I thought you would like to know your friend has decided. I will let her give you the details when she comes home," her lawyer replied.

"Is she gonna take the deal, Amy?"

Amy was smiling into the phone. "Yes, she came to her senses, thank goodness."

Oh, thank you so much. Do you know when she will be home?" Kim asked.

"Hopefully in a few days. We still have to finalize the stipulations, but she made the right choice. She will be doing some work in my office as a condition of probation and to repay her debt. You are a great friend. She told me to tell you that."

Kim thanked Amy again and dialed Marissa. "Pick up, pick up, pick up," Kim repeated as the phone continued to ring. She hung up and texted, "Call me! Great news!" and hit send. Minutes passed with no answer.

"Is Q okay?" Davion asked. "It sounds like good news."

"She is getting out," Kim replied dejectedly.

"Great, but why do you look so sad?" he probed.

"I have been trying to reach Marissa and she's not answering," Kim explained.

She was worried for both friends. Kim felt like she was failing her friend Marissa. Now she had no idea where she was or if she was all right.

"Don't worry. She's probably just out having a good time," Davion said.

"I've always been able to reach her before, and lately she's not calling me back."

"She's probably fine," Davion comforted her.

"I really hope so," Kim confessed, with the knot in her stomach growing.

Chapter 25

It had been two days since Kim heard from Amy Joseph, and today was the day Quaneisha was finally coming home. Kim still had not been able to reach Marissa. She called her twenty times and stopped by her house twice. Her foster mother wasn't too happy either time.

Kim thought about her last visit to Marissa's house.

"Miss Ella, is Marissa home?" Kim asked.

"No," Miss Ella answered.

"Do you know when she'll be back?" Kim pried.

"No, I don't, and my patience is wearing thin with that child. Look, I don't have time to be talking to you. I'm late for my doctor's appointment."

"Oh, okay, I'm sorry to have bothered you,"

Kim replied.

"Look, you seem like a nice kid," Miss Ella said with a sigh. "Why you want to hang around with that bad seed is beyond my understanding. I haven't seen Marissa in two days, but when I do, I'm gon' tear her a new one. No one disrespects this house. It's my rules or the highway, and she is headed toward the highway," she said, with her hands on her hip. "Quaneisha will be home tomorrow afternoon, though. She'll be alright as long as she stays away from her family."

Those were the most words their foster mother had said to Kim all summer. Her news was bittersweet. One friend was coming home and the other was missing. And her foster mom hadn't seen her in two days. Anxiety shot through Kim. She wanted to ask Miss Ella if she'd called the police but felt that was more information than she could ever expect. She suppressed her additional questions and went home, worrying that her friend might be in trouble.

At least now she would get to see Quaneisha, but for Kim the reunion felt a little incomplete: one person was missing. Marissa had been fine until she met her gang banging new boyfriend. No man was worth losing your place to live. He seemed to be total bad news. Hopefully, Quaneisha would get through to Marissa where Kim had failed.

Texting Marissa had been useless, and she had not been at any of the usual hangouts, like the park or dance class. Kim looked at her phone. She had ten minutes to get ready for her swim lesson.

Kim dressed in a pink two-piece, tankini swimsuit that Allison brought home for her the night before, and a pair of jean shorts. She was late for her session with Davion. Kim grabbed her phone and headed for the door. Just as she was about to turn the doorknob, her phone beeped twice.

"Come outside," a new text message read.

Kim ran outside. Quaneisha stood in her driveway, smiling. They hugged each other.

"Q!" Kim screamed.

"Girl, you're a maniac. Who does that? You saved my life. I'm so speechless."

"I'm so happy to see you. I was so afraid that no one would help us," Kim replied.

"You didn't give up!" Quaneisha exclaimed, wiping a tear from her eyes. "No one cared, but you. I don't have words for how grateful I am to you."

"Friends are there through good and bad. I know what it feels like to need some help. I'm just happy that you're out. You didn't deserve to be there."

"I made a stupid mistake. You know my father wanted me to take the wrap for him, because he said I would have done time in juvenile hall and that was cake compared to prison," Quaneisha added. "Why would anyone want their child to go to jail?"

"Sometimes parents act stupid," Kim responded.

Quaneisha smiled. "Real stupid."

"I went by your house yesterday looking for Marissa. Have you heard from her?" Kim asked.

"Yeah, she called me back a few minutes ago. Her new boyfriend is dropping her off in about thirty minutes. I can't wait to see her. I've missed you guys. How's practice going?" Quaneisha asked.

"It is going well. Marissa has been M.I.A. for a few days though. I've called and texted her, but I guess she was too busy with her new man to call me back. I feel better since you heard from her, though. I was really worried," Kim replied.

"What do you mean M.I.A.?" Quaneisha asked.

"Your foster mom told me she hasn't been home in a few days. She missed practice, she hung up on me a few days ago, and I haven't talk to her since that day. She hasn't been around since she met her new guy. Plus, he is in a gang, and I don't know if she's safe with him. I have a real bad feeling about him," Kim said.

"I will set her straight. Her family has strong ties with the Mexican gangs. However, she isn't joining any gang. A gang killed my cousin. He joined it in high school. He made me promise that I would never get involved with gangs," Quaneisha informed her.

"Yeah, we'll get all that sorted out. For now, I'm so happy you're home, Q," Kim beamed.

"Me too!" her friend responded. "Hey, where were you going in that swimsuit?"

"Oh, I forgot. I have swim lessons, and I'm late. Come meet my instructor real quick."

Kim grabbed Quaneisha by the hand and the two friends jogged to Davion's backyard. "Hey, I'm here. Sorry, I'm late, but I got a surprise," Kim said, as she reached Davion.

"I thought you overslept. I was just about to text you," Davion replied.

"This is my friend Quaneisha. She surprised me. Q, this is my friend, Davion. He's teaching me how to swim," Kim said, grinning hard.

"Sweet," Quaneisha responded, smiling at Kim. "Nice to meet you."

"It is nice to finally meet you too," Davion responded. "Are you swimming today, Kim?"

"Yes, I'm ready," Kim replied. "Q, do you want to watch?" Kim asked.

"No, I'm meeting up with Marissa, but I'll call you later. Enjoy your lesson," Quaneisha smiled.

Kim hugged her friend one more time. As

Quaneisha headed out the gate, she gave Kim the thumbs up sign.

"That's the friend you have been talking about?"

"Yep, she just got home today."

"That's so cool," Davion replied. "Hey, I don't think I have time for a full session today. My mom made me an appointment for a physical for football, and it's at eleven. Maybe we can get in thirty minutes," Davion explained.

"Let's skip it then. I don't want you to be late because of me. We can resume tomorrow."

"Okay, sounds good. I just got invited to a beach party tomorrow evening. Do you want to go with me?" he asked.

"I'd love to. Let me ask permission, and text you later," Kim replied.

"Have you thought about the question I asked you the other night at the movies?"

"What question?"

"About becoming my girlfriend," he answered.

Kim wished Davion hadn't brought the subject up. She really liked him, but how could she give him an answer? Her life was in turmoil and she didn't even know where she would be in two weeks. "But I don't know what the future holds for me. I'll probably be leaving in two weeks. It's not fair to you to be involved with someone who isn't around."

"Have you talked to Allison about staying here?" he asked.

"Not yet," Kim answered.

"Then reconsider my offer. You can give me the answer in two weeks."

"You're persistent," she replied.

"I am when I want something. Text me later," Davion replied.

Kim knew she didn't have to worry too much about a decision, because in two weeks she would be headed back to Texas. Davion would find someone else. She felt a small twinge of pain at the thought of Davion talking to someone else. It felt selfish to hold onto him when she didn't know what her future held, but she really liked him. If she was going to choose a boyfriend, it would be someone like him. At the same time, she was afraid a title would end the friendship they'd built. And then she wondered, would Davion change if their relationship changed?

Kim remembered her first crush on the boy from school in Texas. He demanded sex, and when Kim didn't deliver, he lied to his friends and everyone at school, telling them she had sex with him. How did she know Davion wouldn't want sex too? She wasn't ready for that yet. She didn't even know herself anymore, or where her home was. So much had changed for her this summer, she hadn't caught up yet. And, now that Kevin was angry with her, she had no one to talk to about relationships. Staying just friends was sounding better and better, Kim thought as she walked home.

While she walked next door, Kim texted Allison, asking if she could go to the party with Davion the next day, then texted Davion when she got the green light. Just as she grabbed for the door, her cell phone beeped again.

"Meet me at the park," Quaneisha texted.

Chapter 26

Kim's instincts told her something was wrong. She felt utter terror as she ran to the park. Her legs were burning from the exertion, sweat dripping down her forehead. Jitters buzzed through her system as she stumbled over the sidewalk. Her friend had to be all right. They had been through so much drama getting Quaneisha back, and now, life had to settle back down.

Marissa had to be fine. Maybe she had a fight with Carlos, Kim thought, which could be upsetting. Maybe this really wasn't an emergency. Kim turned left, then right, trying to find her friends, but she didn't see then. Then she spotted a shadow next to a picnic table to the far right of the park.

As she got closer to the shadow, the outline of Quaneisha came into focus. She was shielding someone, but Kim couldn't make out the person. Kim's vision tunneled on her friend and all outside noises ceased, as if she were in a hollow tube. Panting, Kim stopped in front of her friends, bent down, placing her hands on her knees to catch her breath. Her sprint had left her. Shaking off her cloudy head, she looked at Quaneisha, who glanced back, and then moved to allow Kim a view of Marissa.

Kim gasped, then stuck her fist in her mouth to prevent the scream she wanted to unleash. Marissa looked like a prizefighter who had just lost a match. The red and black swollen baseball on the right eye offset the golf ball on her left forehead.

Kim grabbed Marissa's right hand and squeezed it, while Quaneisha held the left one. It's Carlos, Kim thought immediately. He had beaten Marissa up. Kim knew he was no good. No member of any gang was ever good. Who beat on a girl who was supposed to be their girlfriend? This guy was a total jerk. Kim wanted to ask Marissa questions, but the air between them was heavy, so the three friends sat quietly.

One single tear slipped down Marissa's swollen cheek, as she closed her eyes tight. "I missed you so much, Q. I just needed somebody," Marissa stammered.

"I missed you too," Quaneisha replied.

"My mother called me with some BS about getting her shit together, and she said she heard I was hanging out with the homies from Encanto and that I should join up with them. All she wanted to talk about was the benefits of joining the gang. I had no one, and I thought it would be great to have a family of people watching your back. You know," Marissa said, as she looked at Quaneisha.

Then she turned toward Kim. "Kim, I'm

sorry I didn't call you back. Things just seemed to be going so well, and I knew you were gonna tell me to stay away from Carlos."

Kim shook her head. "No one was banning you," she told her friend, as she remembered that snake Andrea, taunting her friends on their last visit to the house.

Andrea had even told her mom that Kim was associating with trouble. Andrea was the reason her friend didn't call her back. Kim was seething with anger.

"Carlos's friends wanted me to join the gang, but Carlos didn't. He said that he liked me because I wasn't a part of the negative energy that the gang brought with it. Turns out, he wanted out of the gang. He had applied to join the Navy and was leaving town in a few days. That's why I stayed a few days with him.

"I am so stupid. Carlos left to get us some breakfast. I thought it was him ringing the doorbell, but it was his friend, so I let him in," Marissa said, squeezing Kim and Quaneisha's hands. "I thought no big deal. His eyes were blood shot. He socked me in the face several times, and I fell. He kicked me in the chest, saying, 'Bitch, you're the reason I'm losing my brother.' Then he took out his gun and pointed it at me," she sobbed. "Carlos came in and started yelling. 'What are you doing to my girl? Don't touch her.'

He helped me up and told me to leave. He got between me and his friend, placed the car keys in my hand, and said I should wait at the park. It all happened so fast. I did what Carlos told me, and as I ran out the door, I heard shots. Then I heard his friend crying out, "No, no, I didn't want to hurt you."

Kim felt the horror of Marissa's story. The same chills ran through her body as on that lonely night when her drunken father was passed out in the living room and allowed her room to be invaded by his drunk friend. Kim had narrowly escaped that night with a bat and some quick thinking. She understood the fear and pain Marissa had experienced firsthand.

Marissa took a deep breath and started talking again.

"I abandoned Carlos, but I was scared his friend would come after me next," Marissa said, shaking her head. "I have to believe he's alright. I was so stupid to let his friend in." Marissa winced.

Her breathing slowed, as she gathered more strength to talk. This story was heavy, and the air around them felt thick with sadness and pain.

"Carlos was the only person who seemed to care about me besides you two," Marissa continued. "He even said we could move in together after he finished boot camp. I've got to see if he is okay."

Marissa started sobbing earth-shaking tears. Her friends hugged her, lending their strength and support. Both Quaneisha and Kim were crying, though they both remained silent, letting Marissa work though the horror movie she was reliving. No one had the courage to stop her or ask any questions. How could someone survive that kind of violence? Should they call a doctor or the police?

No one tells you candy causes cavities or smoking causes cancer when you start eating sweets or smoking cigarettes. The advertising makes it look enticing. Marissa's mother made the gang look like a long-lost family reunion, and she had bought it. Marissa thought she was safe with Carlos and his friends, but even Carlos wasn't safe.

Kim was lost in the story, wondering what she could do to help her friend. She blinked back the ache in her chest for her friend and held onto Marissa's hand. She wanted to help her get through this.

"I ache all over, and I don't know where to go. Carlos's friend—the one who beat me up—knows where I live."

Kim stood and started pacing. She glanced nervously around the park, suddenly feeling exposed. "We need to get you inside the house, before he comes by here," Kim responded.

"Right," Quaneisha seconded.

Kim and Quaneisha each put an arm around Marissa's shoulders and helped her walk to exit the park. The sidewalk was only twenty feet away, but the distance seemed like miles.

Each step Marissa took was slow and laborious. She took a step and her balance faltered, Kim and Quaneisha offering support to steady her. When Kim checked their progress, the sidewalk looked even further away. She wished they could carry their friend, but neither girl had the strength. Kim watched the sweat drip down Marissa's forehead; with each step she groaned from the pain. Then Kim noticed the blood dripping down on Marissa's shorts. "Did the bullet hit you too," Kim asked.

"I don't think so. I'm just hurt from the fight. I feel burning pain from where he kicked me. Just need to get home and rest," Marissa responded, as she gritted her teeth. She tried to increase her pace, but her body didn't respond.

They continued at Marissa's pace, glancing around the park, holding hands until they reached Miss Ella's house.

"I messed up real bad," Marissa said, as she hugged Kim. "I'm sorry I didn't listen."

"I find it hard to do sometimes myself. I'll call you guys later," Kim replied as she headed home.

She felt tired and thirsty, and understood Marissa's need for family. Her father was using that need to get her back to Texas. Kim couldn't forget how that need landed her alone in the dark at the house in Texas waiting for her father to pay the bills or buy food. It hurt when people you cared about let you down.

Kim continued down the long hill, and turned the corner, heading up the block to her temporary home. She wanted to shower and go to bed. The heat and her friend's story had drained all her energy. Kim looked up the street as she rounded the corner leading to the house. Why do I feel so awful? she wondered, remembering she had skipped lunch. Kim ate dinner and went to bed.

Kim woke up groggy to sound of her phone chiming.

"I'll pick u up at 4," Davion texted.

Kim had slept the whole night, and half of the day away. She had gotten permission for this party when she first left Davion yesterday, before she had seen Marissa at the park. After hearing Marissa's horrific story, Kim had forgotten about the beach party, and now she didn't think she would enjoy herself. She kept picturing Marissa's mangled face. If she was having a hard time with it, then Marissa had to be going crazy. Kim wanted to go with Davion, but now she didn't know if she would be any fun.

"Everything okay?" he texted back after Kim didn't responded within a few minutes.

Kim thought more about Davion and how much he had done for her, and how excited he seemed about the party.

"I'll be ready," Kim replied, not wanting to disappoint Davion. He had been a gem the whole summer. Maybe they could stay at the party for a short while.

Kim walked into the kitchen and grabbed an apple on her way to the shower. After showering, she lay down for a few minutes before getting dressed. Kim awakened to Andrea's iPod, which she docked on the speakers next to the bed, blasting an explicit lyric rap song.

Kim sighed and looked at the time—she had thirty minutes to get ready for her date with Davion. She jumped up, grabbed the bed for balance, feeling like she had gotten off a merry-go-round too quickly. Once the room stopped moving, she went to her drawers to find some clothes.

Kim grabbed her pink bikini and put a white mini skirt over her bottoms. She went into the bathroom to brush her teeth and splash water on her face. She looked at the reflection staring at her in the mirror. Her narrow face had filled in since her arrival in San Diego and even though her eyes were a little puffy from the need for more sleep, she looked healthy.

Kim brushed her hair, pulling it up into a ponytail, letting her natural curls hang. She walked back to the room and then noticed Andrea putting on makeup in the mirror. She was wearing a bikini, too. Kim hoped they were not going to the same party; getting ignored at home was bad, but in public it would be a real pain. As she walked toward the front door, her phone beeped.

"Hey Kim, are you okay? I haven't heard from you since I gave you the news about your, Dad," Keith texted.

"I'm good," she texted back.

"I was worried. You are so far away that I can't run by and check on you. I miss our long talks," he replied.

"Me too," Kim texted back. She remembered the many nights they had dinner and sat and talked for hours. He totally understood her. He supported her dreams and always made her feel safe.

"The selfish me wants you to come back," Keith responded.

"I'm outside," Davion interrupted with his text.

"K," she texted to Davion.

"Can we talk later?" she replied to Keith.

She closed the door, smiling. Keith wanted her to come back.

Seeing her, Davion smiled as she walked to his car, a Mustang. Same kind of car as Keith, but different colors; same type of guys but different, Kim thought, as she closed the car door.

Davion was speaking, but her head was buzzing with Keith.

"Hey, thanks for coming," Davion said, "My boy Kellen is real people. I want you to meet him."

She nodded, trying to pay attention. Her head still felt fuzzy and the apple had not filled her empty stomach.

"Where's his party, again?" Kim asked.

"It's at Mission Bay. They are grilling some burgers, and each person is bringing a side dish. My mom made a fruit salad for me. Some of the people from my party will be there too."

"Oh, okay," Kim replied, realizing she would not know anyone at this party. At least last time her brother had been there. "Andrea will probably be there with Shea since she and Kellen are cousins," Davion said.

Kim nodded. This was great- Andrea would be there to totally ignore or humiliate her, depending on her mood. Kim wondered why she agreed to go to this party. It was turning out to be a real bad idea, but it was a little too late to change her mind.

"How far away is it?" she asked.

"Ten to fifteen more minutes," he smiled.

It's definitely too late to back out, she thought

195

"Don't worry, it'll be fun," he said reassuringly.

Famous last words, she thought.

Chapter 27

They had been riding for thirty minutes, silently. Davion seemed to understand that she needed some quiet time. It was always perfect how Davion read her. She looked at his perfect white teeth and golden smile. It should be illegal to be so cute.

Once again, his clothes were perfect: blue tank with blue and white board shorts, simple but perfect.

How could there be two perfect guys? Keith was perfect, too. She forced her breath out, as she thought about that smile and dimples. He knew her well too, and he had seen her at her worst and he still came back.

Kim turned her head slightly toward Davion.

Would he run when he learned about her past?
Would he have noticed her in her holey tattered
clothes? He was attracted to an illusion, not the real
Kim from Omaha, Texas.

He bounced his head to the beat playing on
his stereo.

"Thanks again for coming," Davion broke the
uneasy silence.

Kim nodded. What could she say? She
would have felt awful if she'd turned him down. It
was the least she could do. It was the last place she
wanted to be today. How could she be happy, when
her friend was suffering? It was best to remain quiet.

"No sweat," Kim said quietly.

"Are you feeling alright? You seem a million
miles away."

"I'm good. I just feel bad for my friends.
They've both been through a lot in the past few
days," Kim answered.

"You are a great friend. Today give yourself a
break. It is okay for you to have a little fun," Davion
responded smiling.

Those perfect white teeth again. Kim smiled
back at him. Davion rolled down the windows. Kim
inhaled the salt breeze and relaxed into the moment.
As the car rolled to a stop, Kim eyes gravitated to the
huge roller coaster.

"I wanted to show you this side of the beach
before we met my friends. This roller coaster is the
Big Dipper. My stepfather says he used to ride it as a
kid," Davion said, pulling Kim by the hand toward
the amusement park.

"It is huge," Kim replied, watching as the
roller coaster whipped around the curves taking the
screams farther and farther away. Kim had never
seen one this big.

"Let's ride it," he said, pulling her toward the

ticket line. The line moved quickly, moving them closer and closer toward the front of the line. "It's been a long time since I rode it. When I was younger, I rode it every summer."

"I've never ridden one before," Kim responded. Her eyes were glued to the huge structure. "It looks scary."

"Don't worry, it's fun."

Kim watched all the small kids exiting, in one piece, laughing. She looked up, following the height of the roller coaster until it looked like it was touching the clouds. Was it the same height as an airplane? No, it wasn't that high, Kim blinked clearing her vision.

The line moved closer, Kim wanted to build a little more confidence, but her time was running out. Maybe she could wait for Davion on the other side of the ride.

"Don't worry, I'll take care of you," Davion reassured her.

They entered the center seat on the ride, locking the metal bar down. The slow descent up was fun. Kim smiled at Davion, and then her stomach left her body when the roller coaster flew down the first hill. Kim screamed and squeezed Davion's hand harder, as he laughed throwing his other hand in the air. It felt like flying through the air. Kim started laughing too.

This is great, she thought, and then it was over. Kim pulled down her skirt, walking a little shaky from the ride.

"Come on, I smell cotton candy. Wanna share some?" he asked. The pink cotton candy was passed between them back and forth, as they walked toward the boardwalk. "Let's sit for a minute on the retaining wall."

The sand started on the other side of the

three-foot retaining wall. The beach was covered with people, tanning, swimming, running, playing Frisbee, from young to old. The clear blue sky seemed to end in the deep blue ocean.

"It's beautiful," Kim said.

"Close your eyes and listen for a minute. This is my favorite part," Davion instructed her.

Kim closed her eyes, trying to tune out the laughter and voices. The soft roaring waves were powerful and relaxing. The crash of the waves hitting the rocks felt like a cup of hot chocolate, soothing. Kim opened her eyes and watched the waves roll in, enjoying the peace she felt. Kim wiped the sweat as it beaded on her forehead.

He leaned in closer, "At night the sound is ten times more powerful." He pulled the fallen strands of hair away from her face. "Let's walk down the boardwalk to the party."

Kim opened her eyes looking into Davion's brown ones, shivering from the heat generated from the proximity. She turned her head toward the beach again. "Wait, can we walk down the beach instead?"

He answered by leading her through the opening in the retaining wall. Taking off her flip-flops, she got her footing in the warm granules of sand that slipped between her toes, avoiding the pieces of trash littered around the beach. This day was brightening. She was having so much fun. Kim would have never thought she could see past the storm clouds hovering over her, but Davion brought the sunshine. He seemed to just blend well with her. Why would any girl not want to hang with him? He was a total package. If she was staying in San Diego, Kim might consider his request. Spending time with him made her feel warm on the inside like her mother's cooking used to do. It filled you up and left you feeling totally satisfied.

Kim's terry cloth skirt buzzed. Kim took out her phone.

"Call me. More news," Keith texted.

"K," she texted back. There was her other problem: Keith. He came into her life when she was alone, and filled a void. And those dimples. That smile. He was the total package.

Just when Kim thought Keith was the only guy she would feel butterflies and electric tingles for, Davion walked into her life, bringing butterflies, tingling sensations, and swim lessons.

As they walked closer to the end of the path leading back to the boardwalk and grassed area Kim noticed the crowd of multi-colored bikinis barely covering skin. She felt overdressed.

The closer they got to the crowd, the louder the music and laughter seemed. It was like a concert—minus the music blaring out of black speakers sporting the words "Bose."

Kim inhaled the smoky sweet smell of barbeque. Her nose followed the scent until she spotted the grill and picnic table holding the buffet. Unfortunately, she was being led in the opposite direction, toward the center of the dancing crowd. Her mouth felt like the sand she had been walking on. She needed a drink.

"Hey, can we get water?" Kim asked, pulling Davion to a stop.

"Okay, just a second," he answered, detouring to a blue tub stationed to the right of the dancing bodies.

Fishing the water out of the icy bucket, he handed Kim the water.

Kim opened the bottle, drinking the liquid in three swallows and she still felt thirsty and now a little light-headed. Dumping the empty bottle in the metal trash can, they headed back toward the dance floor.

The music and the crowd were closing in around her, making her feel like a kid on a runaway merry-go-round, and she needed to get off the ride.

Davion noticed the distressed look on her face.

"I just want you to meet my best friend. He's my boy. Then I'll get us out of this." Davion walked over to chocolate tall guy sporting shades and board shorts, dancing in the center of five girls, all working their bodies to beat of the music. "Hey Vince!" Davion yelled.

His friend made eye contact and started moving his little crowd toward them. Everyone kept moving with the music, even though they were now traveling.

"Hey, man! Glad you made it," Vince responded.

"Cool, I wouldn't miss your day. I want you to meet Kim," Davion replied.

"Hey Kim. Enjoy yourself, get some food. My moms threw down. I'll catch up with you guys in a few," Vince responded.

"Do your thing. We will be around," Davion said, as they bumped fists.

Davion led Kim out of the crowded dancing bodies and back to the table of food. Kim stomach growled.

"My stomach is in agreement with yours," he laughed.

"I am starving. And I haven't had barbeque in a while," Kim said. "They're a pretty big deal in Texas."

"Well, hopefully this one stacks up alright, Texas girl."

Kim smiled weakly, then started piling the food on her plate. Baked beans, potato salad, mac, and cheese; then hot links and chicken breast. They headed for an open spot of grass.

"Your plate looks light in comparison to mine," Kim said.

"I'm pacing myself because I want a piece of Vince's mom's Ooey Gooey cake. It is delicious," Davion replied, licking his lips.

Kim laughed between bites of food. The dizziness and fuzzy feeling was still there. "His mom made all this food?" Kim asked.

"I think so. She is always feeding the guys and me when we visit his place. Everything she touches is good, even the toast."

"Well the food is great," Kim responded, looking up at Davion. Then she noticed a familiar pink bikini. "Oh wonderful," she sarcastically sighed.

Davion turned and followed her field of vision to Andrea. "You guys still have issues?"

"Issues, yeah that's a word I would think of to describe our problems. I can't breathe right for her," Kim replied, looking away from the pink bikini moving into the crowd of dancing bodies.

"Don't let her spoil your night," Davion consoled.

"I'll try," Kim replied, knowing that is just what happened.

The dizziness was now making her feel shaky, and she could not drink enough; but she didn't want to spoil Davion's night with her complaining so she smiled.

Meanwhile she started enjoying four other couples doing a synchronized routine like the movie "Step Up." Kim enjoyed watching the dance change with the various beats. Davion pulled her onto the grassed dance area to dance with him through a few songs, until his friend brought him two pieces of that Ooey Gooey cake.

"Moms wanted to make sure you got some

cake because it's about to be gone," Vince said, giving another fist pound.

"Good looking out," Davion replied, giving Kim a bite. "You have to try this."

"He must really like you," Vince said with a laugh, "because he doesn't share that cake with anyone."

Kim blushed and bit down on a sweet slice of heaven.

"Wow, this is amazing. I don't think I have ever tasted a cake like this."

"Yeah, it's one of my mom's best recipes. Enjoy!" Vince replied.

"Thank you," Kim said, savoring each bite of the crumb, custard cake.

"Man did you see that girl in the pink bikini that was dancing near me?" Vince asked.

"Who, Andrea?" Davion replied.

"You know her? Please introduce us. She's a hottie," Vince salivated.

"That would be Kim's stepsister," Davion responded, as both sets of eyes settled on Kim.

"Introduce me…please." Vince repeated.

"I'll see what I can do," Davion responded, taking the awkward moment way from Kim.

Kim searched for her roomie, who seemed to be hugging herself like something was out of place. Kim couldn't fight the urge to find out why anything would make Andrea feel uneasy. She started heading toward Andrea, Davion followed. When Kim got close enough, she could see the fear in Andrea's eyes. Kim needed to understand why, so she continued forward.

"Hey Andrea!" Kim yelled.

Andrea's loud friend answered, "We don't know you!" she slurred. "Girl, come on. Let's go. I have some place I need to be," Shea said, as her alcohol breath introduced itself before she finished her sentence.

"Hey, I came over because Vince wants to meet you," Kim responded.

"We are leaving!" Shea yelled.

"We'll drop her off. You go ahead," Davion piped in.

"I'll stay, Shea. I'll call you tomorrow," Andrea replied.

"You sure, I know you can't stand that man-stealing, country thang," Shea replied, pointing at Kim.

"Maybe you need to find a designated driver," Davion said, pulling Kim away from Andrea's loud friend.

"Thanks for that," Andrea responded toward Davion.

"Thank Kim. She's the one who intervened," Davion replied.

They briefly looked at each other, Kim glancing away first. Shea had just added another layer to the mean, nasty attitude Andrea had been throwing at her all summer. It was obvious she thought Kim was beneath her.

"Don't worry I will only be sharing your space a few more weeks," Kim informed her.

Andrea for once remained silent.

"Andrea, my boy Vince. Vince, this is Andrea," Davion introduced, as they stepped into the crowd that was dancing around his friend.

Andrea looked shocked that she was really being introduced to the birthday boy.

"How long are you going to be here?" he asked.

Looking at Davion, Andrea answered, "I don't know."

Davion looked at Kim. "Hey you okay?" he

asked.

"I'm not feeling so good," Kim answered. Shea's nasty comments seemed to take the last little bit of energy from Kim. Her head felt like it wanted to explode, and stars were circling her head. Davion's voice seemed a mile away and her skin felt cold.

"Man, we are going to have to head out. Kim is not looking so good," Davion said.

"Sit here for a few minutes while I run get the car," Davion said, as he started jogging in the direction of the car.

Kim heard Vince talking to Andrea, exchanging numbers, laughing like old friends. Kim wanted to warn him that Andrea was a wolf in a pink bikini, but she didn't have the energy. Her main focus was staying awake until Davion returned with the car. The table kept moving like it had wheels. She kept hearing the voices trying to stay focused on the voices, but her vision was fading with the voices. Maybe she could just lie down until Davion got back with the car. A little nap might help the spinning and the voices stop.

Chapter 28

Sirens and voices were what Kim woke up to, and someone holding her arm.

"Ouch," she mouthed, as the words seemed to stop at her vocal cords.

Kim opened her eyes and turned her head to the right. She saw clear plastic metal trimmed cabinets filled with medical supplies. She turned her head to a voice on the left, where a blonde lady in a blue uniform with soft green eyes was sitting on a black bus bench seat speaking and taping a tube to her arm. Kim tried to lift her arm, but it fell back to her side. Blinking, she tried to focus on the green-eyed woman next to her.

"Do you remember what happened?" the green-eyed lady asked.

Kim shook her head.

"We are taking you to the hospital. You passed out. Have you done anything like this before?" she asked.

Her head shook once again.

"Your parents will meet us there," green eyes said.

"ETA five minutes!" the voice from the front yelled.

The lady squeezed Kim's hand. "We are going to take care of you."

Kim blinked back a few tears, closed her eyes and tried to stop her hands from shaking. What had happened at the beach? She remembered Andrea waiting with her for Davion to go get the car, and now she was laid out in an ambulance. Kim gagged and spit into a pink kidney shaped basin, as a wave of nausea made the ambulance ride feel like a choppy boat ride.

The green-eyed blonde started talking again as she wheeled her into the hospital emergency room.

"Teenage female, collapsed at a beach party, altered level of consciousness, she was out for about ten minutes. Vitals, temp 97.6, pulse 120, resp 20, and B/P 124/66. No c/o pain or discomfort, responds to verbal commands. Her family is en route."

"Place her in Bay 1," a nurse said.

"I want CBC, Chem 20, EKG, and CT on call in case we need them. What is her name?" a doctor asked.

"Kim," the green-eyed blond responded.

"Kim, I am Dr. John Jones. Can you hear me?"

"Yes," Kim whispered.

"Do you know what happened?" he asked.

Kim shook her head.

"Are you in pain?" Dr. Jones asked.

"Achy all over," she answered.

208

"Has this ever happened before?"

"No," Kim replied.

"Look at the light. Follow it with your eyes only. How do you feel?" the doctor asked.

"I'm tired and I feel like I swallowed cotton. I want to sle…," Kim slurred, as she passed out again.

The voices faded into the background; a little more sleep was what she needed. Everyone was talking to her and asking questions, and she did not feel like answering any more questions. If they let her sleep, then she would answer their questions.

"Here she is," Dr. Jones said.

A warm hand gently squeezed Kim hand, "Kim, honey are you okay?" Allison asked.

"Yes, I'm good. Just tired," Kim whispered.

She remembered the comfort she felt in her mother's touch. She was happy to share that connection with Allison. Kim wanted to keep that feeling forever. It had been too long since she felt that way.

"Have you ever done this before?" Allison asked.

"No," Kim answered. "I just need to rest."

"Doctor, do you know what's wrong?" Allison raised her head and turned toward Dr Jones.

"We drew some blood. I am waiting on the results. Do you have a family history of anything like this?" he inquired.

"Kim's adopted and we don't have a family history on her biological family," Allison responded.

Kim winced.

"We will have some answers when the labs come back. Her EKG was normal, and I am sending her to have a CT scan now. Don't worry, we're going to get to the bottom of this," Dr. Jones reassured them.

Robert walked up the white tiled floors and

placed an arm around his wife. "Are you okay?" he asked.

Closing her eyes from the bright white lights, she nodded.

Kim shivered.

"The doctor has run some tests and they are waiting on the results. She is headed to get a CAT scan. She looks so pale. Maybe she is just dehydrated," Allison responded.

"We will get to the bottom of it," Robert said. He squeezed his wife's shoulder and the hand that surrounded Kim's.

Blinking back tears, Kim remembered the day she got a tooth pulled and her coach took her to the dentist, because her father was nowhere to be found. He missed so much of her life since her mother died. You needed parents to be there when a storm hit. Kim's storm was hitting, and Kevin's parents were here to help her through it.

She closed her eyes to stop the white room from spinning. They released her hand, and Kim felt cold and alone. This was her reality, she thought as the gurney headed for the CT scan.

"We will wait here," Robert said.

Allison nodded. "Kim, don't worry. We're not going anywhere."

"Thank you," Kim whispered.

Maybe the cold feelings would recede when she was brought back to the room that they warmed. Kim closed her eyes to shut out the white lights and tan walls. The bumpy ride ended in a small room. They placed Kim in the center of a large, white, donut-shaped contraption.

The machine-made beeping noises. "Please keep real still," the tech announced.

Kim was returned to the emergency room, where the room was filled with her temporary family and Davion. Julian spoke up. "Are you okay?"

Kim smiled. "I've felt better."

"You guys have seen her now go back in the waiting room," Allison said.

"Mom, can I talk to her a minute alone, please?" Andrea asked.

"Honey, she is tired. Can it wait?" Allison said.

Kim hoped it could wait; she was too tired for any confrontation with Andrea. Nothing she attempted had broken through the barrier Andrea had built. Kim didn't have the energy to hit her head against that concrete wall anymore. When she got better it would be time to leave, and Andrea could wallow in her selfishness.

"Mom, I need to do it now, please," Andrea pleaded.

"Five minutes. She needs to rest," Allison relented.

"Thanks, I'll make it quick," she replied.

Kim raised her eyebrows. Were those tears in Andrea's eyes?

"I'm so sorry. I have been a total witch this summer. I don't know. I've never had to share before, and it kinda sucks, but you know I never gave it a chance. I didn't deserve your help, but you did it anyway," Andrea blurted out, as she wiped the tears that fell. "I've thought about everything, and I wanted you to know that it's okay with me if you wanna stay. I will try to not be a total jerk about things, as long as you stay out of my things." Andrea turned to leave, "I forgive you for Davion. I guess you didn't know he was supposed to be my Boo. I hope you feel better soon."

Kim watched Andrea leave, closing her mouth. Kim did a mental replay. Was that an apology from her? Was this her way of asking Kim to stay with them? Kim chuckled. Andrea was full of surprises.

The brown curtain opened. Davion walked up to the gurney. "I had to see you before I went home. I was so scared when I returned with the car. You are the first girl that I've met that I have felt so comfortable with. You're just real, from your natural brown curls, to the almond-shaped, brown eyes. You gripped my heart with your conviction for your friends," Davion said, reaching for her hand. "I just wanted you to know that you are special to me, which was why I wanted you to be my girl. Anytime with you would be special for me. Get better so we can finish our swim sessions."

He brought her hand to his lips, placing a gentle kiss there. Kim brushed away the tears. He was so perfect, but he deserved more than she could give him. She couldn't find the words to explain any of this to him. He had rallied behind her the whole summer, coming to her rescue on many occasions. Plus, he was a lot of fun to be around. She was not being fair to him.

"You will be fine." Davion informed her. "Oh yeah I wanted you to know you saved Andrea's butt, too. Shea had been drinking, and she hit a fence and totaled the front of her red BMW. The police were at the scene of her accident when Andrea called 911, so they got there quick. Add her to the list of people whose life you have affected. Here's your phone. I'll check with you tomorrow."

"Thank you for everything, D," Kim whispered. Her phone buzzed, and she looked down and noticed a text from Keith and two missed calls from him too. She looked back at Davion, where the frown on his face showed he had noticed the missed calls. "He just a friend from Texas."

"I wanted you to know how I felt, but if

someone else holds your heart then it makes sense why you can't open it for me." He looked at the floor, turned and left.

Kim's body shook from the ache he left in her heart. He got under her skin even though she wanted to prevent it. The tears kept falling. She couldn't deny his assessment of her, and it was all the truth. He had wriggled away the shell she had built and found a place in her heart; holding onto the past had not prevented it. Both guys were wonderful parts of her life, but she didn't want to give up the past for an uncertain future. It really wasn't fair to Davion. The door opened again, Kim wiped the tears as the doctor walked in with Allison and Robert.

"Kim, I have the results of your tests. I've asked your parents to come in to hear everything. First, you will be okay. Your CT scan was negative for any abnormalities. Your EKG was normal; however, your blood work had a few abnormal results. Your blood glucose level was 864, so we are starting an insulin drip," Dr. Jones informed them. "And you're feeling ill because you have Type 2 Juvenile Diabetes."

Chapter 29

"What does that mean?" Kim asked, wondering if she had heard the doctor correctly.

He said she had diabetes, but that was an old person's disease, not someone her age. None of this made sense. The doctor had to be mistaken. All that happened was that she'd fainted. This did not mean she was sick. They had to run more tests. This could not be right.

"You have juvenile onset diabetes. Diabetes is a disease that prevents the body from using the energy from the food you eat. Your pancreas is an organ that produces insulin, which helps digest your food. Diabetes happens when insulin isn't produced and the pancreas doesn't work," the doctor said. He drew a picture of a pancreas. "Your pancreas isn't producing enough insulin to digest your food, so we will have to give you insulin to help. We will keep you in the hospital a few days to help regulate your blood sugar and teach you how to live with this. You can lead a normal life, and we are here to help you through this transition."

"Doctor, are you sure?" Allison asked. "She seemed fine until today."

"The tests are pretty conclusive. We've been checking her blood sugar, and the results point to diabetes. She will need your help to make this transition. I have a dietician coming up to your room tomorrow to help teach you what to eat," the doctor replied. "I'll check on you later." The doctor smiled and left the room.

"Kim, Robert and I are here to help you," Allison responded.

"We feel like you are already a part of our family," Robert added.

Kim was speechless. She hadn't expected this. They were the best parents a kid could hope for, but she would only be here two more weeks. Her father had been firm about her going back to Texas. But who would help her in Texas?

"Thank you for helping me," she said to Allison and Robert. "I don't know what I'd do without you. And I'm worried about going home at the end of summer; my dad won't understand any of this."

"We'll talk to him," Robert replied.

A small burn started in her chest, radiating out, the warmth moving throughout her body. If felt good to get help from Robert and Allison. They were acting like Kim was a part of the family.

The Admitting Clerk walked into the room.

"Could you fill out the papers for your daughter. We will need a copy of her medical card, and emergency contact information. Do you have hospital copay with your insurance?" the clerk asked.

"Kim is with us for the summer. We will contact her father and get you the information you need," Allison replied.

"I will leave the forms, so you can fill them out. I will be back in thirty minutes to pick them up," the clerk said, as she walked toward the door.

"Thank you," Allison responded.

"I don't have insurance," Kim responded.

"It is okay. Let us talk to your father and then we will work something out," Allison replied. "What is his number?"

Kim sat up on her gurney. She closed her eyes briefly to the spinning room. "My neighbor Tim will have to get him for you because my dad doesn't have a phone. Will you hand me my phone, please?" Kim scrolled down her list of friends and showed Allison the number.

"Great, let me call him now." Allison punched in the number. "Hello, this is Allison, Kevin's mother, and I needed to reach Francis. Could you see if he is home, please?"

"Are they getting him?" Robert asked. "I'll talk to him when he gets on the phone."

"Tim went to get him," Allison replied, handing the phone to Robert.

"Hello?" Robert said, then he paused to listen. "Okay, please tell him it is important to call us. Yes, that is the number he can reach us at. Have you seen him recently?" Robert asked. "Thank you."

"Had Tim seen my father?" Kim asked.

"Tim said he hadn't seen him in a few days, but he left a note for him," Robert replied.

A young guy in scrubs suddenly walked into Kim's room.

"Hello, I'm here to take you up to your

room." He pulled up the black rails and started pushing the gurney. "You guys can follow me on up. She'll be in room 425."

"Kim, we are going to send the kids home, and we'll be right up," Robert informed her.

Kim laid her head back and closed her eyes to stop the room from spinning. The bumpy ride stopped as they entered the elevator. Alcohol with an antiseptic smell filled the air as she passed the nurse's station on her way to room 425. She settled into her crisp white sheets.

Her father hadn't been seen in a few days. Keith texted her several times, but she hadn't read the messages yet. He was probably trying to tell her something about her father. Kim hoped Francis was doing okay. He didn't take good care of himself, and had no one to help. Maybe she should just go back. He needed her. Kevin's family didn't need her to survive, but Francis did. She had to call Keith; he could go find her father.

Kim picked up her pink phone to read the text from Keith.

"Got some news for you," Keith texted.

Kim typed question mark and sent the text.

Someone knocked on her door interrupting her cyber conversation. "Come in!" Kim yelled.

"Hey, are you alright?" Quaneisha asked.

"Yeah, girl," Kim answered. "How did you find out?"

"I was coming over to talk to you. Kevin told me what happened and offered to bring me over," Quaneisha replied.

"Wow," Kim said.

"He said he would give us some time, and then he would come in and talk to you. He says you have diabetes?"

"Yeah, that's what the doctor tells me."

"I thought only old people got that disease. My foster mom has it, and she says she has to take her medicine so she won't lose her foot. Are you going to lose your foot?" Quaneisha asked.

"I hope not. The doctor didn't say anything about losing my feet," Kim replied.

This was becoming the worst day of her life and her father couldn't be found. Kim wanted to scream at him, but he wouldn't hear her. What she felt didn't matter to him. Why did he even want her back at home?

"Well, maybe only older people lose their feet if they have it," Quaneisha offered, after seeing the distressed look on Kim face. "Don't worry, I'm sure I was mistaken; maybe it was her high blood pressure, or ulcers, or gout. She has so many problems, could be any of the other ones. So how are you feeling?"

Kim wiped a tear that slipped down her face. "I'm doing okay."

"I don't think this is a good time, but I wanted to let you know Marissa is in the hospital too. After we left you, she started coughing up blood and I dialed 911. Miss Ella had a fit about it, saying she wasn't paying any medical bills for an unnecessary ambulance ride," Quaneisha explained. "I am glad I didn't listen to her, because the firefighter said I made a good call. He thought she had some internal bleeding from that beat-down she got at Carlos's place."

"Is she going to be alright?" Kim asked.

"I think so. The paramedic said he would take care of her and she was still talking to me when she left. I think they will stop the bleeding, and then she will come home. My best friends are both in the hospital. That's so crazy."

"Let me know when you find out how she's doing," Kim replied.

"I will, but you worry about you. You've spent too much time worrying about everybody else. Get better so we can hang out. I'm going to see her when I leave here."

"I will," Kim answered. "Thanks for coming to see me, Q."

"You got it, girl. Do you think your father will still make you go home?"

"I don't know. I was too expensive for him before, and now that I'm sick, I don't see how he can handle it. We don't have insurance. I don't know who's going to pay for my medical bills now. I don't want to be a problem for Allison and Robert either," Kim replied.

"Maybe they can get Medi-Cal for you. I have Medi-Cal and it pays for my medical care. Just get better. We can work it off if we need to."

"Have you started working for Amy Joseph yet?" Kim asked, remembering the deal she had made with Quaneisha's lawyer for volunteer services in exchange for free legal aide. "I hope you aren't upset that I made that deal. I actually told her that I'd work it off, but she said you had to do it."

"Nah, it's all good. I need to work it off myself. I start next Saturday. I'm actually looking forward to it. Maybe one day I can be a lawyer and help people who need it. Hey, I'm going to let you rest for now, okay? I'll text you, and if you are still here, I'll come back in a few days. I want to get the bus before it gets too late."

"Text me when you see Marissa, so I know she is alright. The doctor says I only have to stay a few days, so hopefully Marissa will be home by then, too," Kim replied.

Quaneisha hugged Kim and waved when she reached the door.

Kim's phone beeped.

219

"Have you heard from your father?" Keith texted.

"No, but I need to talk to him. Could you go by the house and tell him to call me?" Kim responded.

"Been by the house. No one has seen him. I will go by again today. Don't worry, I will find him. You okay?" Keith texted.

"Yeah. Long story. Will explain later. Please find him," Kim responded.

"I will," Keith sent back.

Kim laid her phone on the nightstand next to her bed. Her world was so messed up. She was sick' and once again, her dad was missing in action. Why did he do this? Did he want her to come home to that mess? She would be alone with no one to help her through this diabetes problem.

Kim hoped Marissa would be okay. Coughing up blood was not good. She needed to get out of this cold white room. She had a missing dad and a sick friend; her diabetes could wait.

Kim closed her eyes and massaged her temples hoping to relieve the ache that was starting behind her eyes.

Chapter 30

Spending the night at the hospital was exhausting. Weird smells and odd noises, this was not a place to rest, Kim decided. The nurses had awakened her every four hours to take her temperature and blood pressure. How did people rest and get better when they didn't let you sleep? Kim jumped every time they pricked her finger to check her blood sugar, which was five times a day if she was lucky, and more often if her blood sugar was too high. The tips of her fingers were sore and achy. She didn't want to do this forever.

This sucks, Kim thought. Why couldn't they invent a pill to fix this? Kim certainly wasn't looking forward to her session with the teacher to learn how to take care of herself. She didn't want to learn how to prick her finger every day. Could they be wrong about her disease? She'd been alright until a few weeks ago, so maybe it was a virus that she just needed to get over.

"Kim, good morning. I am your nurse today and my name is Marie. I have your breakfast. I am going to give you some insulin before you eat and then we will check your blood sugar an hour after you finished. I want you to call me when you finish eating," Marie said. Kim looked up to see Marie walking with a hop in her step, black short-cropped haircut, like a Halle Berry in scrubs. She set down the tray of food on Kim's bedside table and left the room.

It smelled like bacon. Kim lifted the green lid. Scrambled eggs and bacon with one slice of wheat toast sat on the plate. Kim tasted the eggs. It was better than some of the food she had in Texas when her father had forgotten to buy groceries. She picked up the sugar-free grape jelly, peeling the foil lid back; it smelled like grapes. Kim dabbed her finger into the jelly and tasted it, smiled and spread it on her toast. She seasoned her eggs with salt and peppers and ate her breakfast. When she finished, she hit the call light.

Breakfast tasted like a school meal she had eaten every day. Not quite like her mother's cooking, but tasty. Maybe she could do this thing. "I finished my breakfast. Could I have a drink of orange juice?"

"Orange juice has sugar in it, and it would raise your blood sugar too high, so I can't give you that. Would you like some ice water?" Marie asked.

"Yeah," Kim answered, frowning. Man, this really sucks, she thought.

"The diabetes educator will be here at 10 a.m., when your family comes back. She will help you understand everything. It will get easier. I will be back in an hour to check your blood sugar," Marie responded, taking the empty tray away.

Easy for her to say, she wasn't dying of thirst over here, Kim thought, not to mention the promise that she would return to poke and prod Kim more. Kim sighed, pulled her crisp white sheets and blanket up to her chin and turned away from the door to catch a nap. She hit the switch on her hand remote, darkening the room.

It felt like she had just drifted off to sleep, when the door to her room opened, and her phone buzzed on her nightstand. Kim reached for the phone.

"Kim, it is time to check your blood sugar. I brought you a visitor."

When Kim turned toward to face the voice, her brother stood to the side of the nurse. His eyes were glassy and his face was unshaven.

"Let me have a finger," Marie said, reaching for Kim's hand. She scanned her hospital ID, punched in some numbers, and pricked Kim's finger. The number flashed up 118. "That is good; your blood sugar is in the range the doctor wants it. Do you need anything else?"

"No, thank you," Kim closed her eyes. She heard the door open again and the chair slide closer to her bed.

"Kim, I am so sorry," Kevin said as he reached for her hand.

Kim squeezed her brother's hand and opened her eyes. "None of this is your fault."

"It's so different here, Kim," her brother rambled. "I am still trying to fit in. I just don't want to mess up."

"What are you talking about, Kevin?"

"I just wanted things to be perfect for both of us here. I didn't want anything to mess things up," Kevin replied.

"I wasn't trying to mess things up for you. I

didn't come here to make things bad for you," Kim answered. "I'm sorry if I have."

"You haven't done anything wrong. You have made my family complete. A part of our old family, the good part, and my new family combined. I want you to fit in so we both can stay, but I went about it all the wrong way," Kevin replied. "You should have the right to choose your own fate, but I've only wanted the best for you. Remember the hell in Texas? I'll never go back to that. But I respect your right to make your own choice. I know you have your reasons."

"Kevin, Francis wants me to go back. He's the only father I've known, and I love him despite his faults. I don't see any other way," Kim replied.

"You and Francis have always had a special bond. He treated me fine, but he adored you. If he couldn't get his life together for himself, I thought he would do it for you," Kevin said, as he released Kim's hand and walked toward the window and then looked at Kim. "He hasn't changed, and he can't take care of you. I don't wanna lose you like we lost our mother."

Kim watched the tears fall from her brother's eyes. Her own eyes moistened. They both had lost Maggie; she had been a mother to both of them when their biological parents were unable to raise them. Now Kevin's parents had grown and matured and were ready to have him back in their lives. But Kim wasn't ready to discard the things her father had done for her. What about earlier in their life, before Maggie died? He had loved her unconditionally, but that didn't pay the bills. Her father had the final decision, not her. She would have to suffer through his choice.

"I don't get to make the decision."

"Maybe he'll care enough to leave you here. Your health should matter more than his pride,"

Kevin replied.

Kim remained silent. She knew her father wouldn't know what to do for a child with health issues. He fell apart with their mother and left her to Kim and Kevin to care for, so how could he ever care for Kim? She would have to do it all herself. This diabetes thing was scary and now she would have no one to help her. Kim wiped tears from her eye and watched her brother looking out the window.

Kevin sighed. "I also want to apologize for my attitude toward your friends. Quaneisha's a cool person. She just made a mistake and we all make mistakes. I just didn't want you to hang out with the wrong crowd."

"It's nice to hear you say that. I wish you would've trusted my judgment," Kim said. If only he would apply it to their father. Would he ever look past Francis's faults?

"Me too," Kevin whispered. "I'm going to be here to help you though this."

"I'm scared, I've never really been sick before. I don't know if I can do this," Kim replied.

"We can do it together," Kevin answered.

Kim was pleased her brother was stepping up to help, but he wouldn't be in Texas. Her father was too consumed with his self to be there to help her. She needed her mother, but she was gone forever.

Just then, Allison and Robert walked in the room. "Good morning!" they said in unison.

"Good morning!" Kim replied with a smile.

"The educator was out at the desk. She'll be in shortly. We are all here to help you get through this," Allison said looking at Kim, her eyes soft.

As if on cue, the educator walked in with a stack of papers on her clipboard, wearing a white lab coat that read, Dietician M. Love on the patch. Her black heels clicked with each step she took toward the bed.

"Hello, my name is Mandisa, and I'm here to teach you what foods to eat. Let me ask you this to start: What are some of your favorite foods?"

"I like spaghetti and fruits, and some vegetables," Kim replied.

"You can still eat those foods, especially vegetables and some fruits. I'm going to teach you how to look at the labels of the foods you eat. Foods are made of groups of ingredients like recipes you see when you make a dish at home. The label will list the ingredients as well as the amount of carbohydrates that each food contains," she explained. "Your job is to eat foods with low carbohydrate numbers. Carbohydrates raise your blood sugar levels quickly, so you eat small amounts of carbohydrates with each meal and your blood sugar rises a small amount only."

"Should she cut out all carbohydrates?" Allison asked.

"No, she just shouldn't eat large amounts, but she can still have some, like whole-wheat spaghetti in her diet. Here is a list of foods you might normally eat and an exchange food that would be better," the dietician handed a copy to Kim and one to Allison.

"There's a lot of food on this list," Kim commented.

"Yes, there is. Look at this way. You're giving your body healthy fuel. This is an excellent start to healthy eating for you. Think of it as a different way to eat, not impossible. Your doctor will decide on the total carbohydrates you should eat with each meal, and then Allison uses the list to get the food you can eat. Any questions?" the dietician asked.

"Could I ever eat cake or ice cream?" Kim asked.

"Kim, occasionally you can have a small amount of a special treat. There're healthier desserts on the list that you can eat, too. Do you exercise?" she asked.

"Yes, I dance and run," Kim replied.

"Great! Keep exercising. When you do, your body uses more fuel and it lowers your blood sugar and causes your body to use insulin better. Exercise is really important. Read over the material I gave you and I will come and see you later." Then Mandisa the dietician clicked out of the room.

"Kim, this'll help us all eat healthier. We'll help you adjust," Allison responded.

"Thanks," Kim replied. There were pages and pages of food in the brochure. There was even a sugar-free chocolate pudding on the list.

"Kim, all of this is regular food," Kevin said, as he looked over his mother's shoulder.

"I'll go grocery shopping to make sure we have the food you need in the house. The doctor said you could probably go home tomorrow. I still haven't got a hold of Francis, but we'll keep trying. Meanwhile we'll get the house ready for you," Allison responded.

"You just get some rest," Robert said.

"I've got to go into work for a short shift," Kevin told Kim.

"Thanks," Kim replied. She waved to everyone as they exited her room. Kim was happy they all showed up to support her new scary life. But where was her father and why didn't he care enough to call? He wanted her home, so why hadn't he called to demand she come home? Kim didn't know the answers to his disappearance, but she had her own problems to worry about. She was tired, physically and mentally. She hoped she had time for a nap before the next round of poking and prodding.

Chapter 31

Kim woke up early, pulling the white sheets up to cover her chilled arms. She could finally go home. She climbed out of bed and walked over to the window; the sky was lighting. It had been easy to adjust to eating the food the nurses brought, but would she be able to do all the things the nurse had taught her. It just seemed like it was all too much. Kim didn't think she could poke her finger five times a day or give herself injections.

Kim jumped at the sound of her phone buzzing, and quickly grabbed it from the bedside table.

"Hello?" Kim answered.

"Are you alright?" Keith asked.

Kim climbed back under the cold sheets and brought the head of the bed up high. "I am okay. How did you find out?" Kim asked.

"Tim called me after Kevin's mother left the message. He told me you were in the hospital. You know news travels like a wildfire here. Tell me what happened," Keith said.

"They think I have diabetes. I feel fine, just a little tired. Maybe it is just a virus," Kim responded.

"What did the doctor say, Kim?" Keith asked.

"He said I'm a diabetic," Kim answered, rolling her eyes.

"Then you need to do what the doctor says. Listen, when you were given information, what you do with that information will determine what kind of life you have. Hiding from the truth only hurts you," Keith responded.

Kim sighed, and shifted onto her side.

"Promise me you'll do what the doctor tells you to do," Keith said.

"It isn't that serious. I mean, you're acting like I got into an accident or something," Kim responded.

"Promise me," Keith repeated.

"Alright," Kim conceded.

"You have to take care of yourself. The diabetic people who take care of themselves live normal lives. The people who act like they don't have it develop complications from it, like poor circulation. My uncle lost his foot because he didn't listen. I don't want to see you like him," Keith explained.

"Wow, are you serious?" Kim sat up higher in the bed.

"Very serious. I'm not trying to fuss at you. I just want you to take this seriously," Keith responded. "Now enough of that. I've been trying to locate your father, but I'm having a little difficulty. Don't worry, he is not in any of the hospitals, so I think he's with one of his friends."

Kim let out the breath she had been holding.

She needed her father and he was still missing. She should be worried about herself and how to deal with learning her new lifestyle, but all she could think about was her father. He didn't have a good track record of taking care of himself.

"Are you sure he's alright?"

"Well, I know he's not in any of the hospitals. You concentrate on getting healthy and let me take care of finding your father. I'll find him. Trust me," Keith reassured her.

"Thank you," Kim said.

"You're welcome. I'll call you when I know something."

Kim hung up the phone. Thousands of miles away from her father, and she still was being affected by him. Where could he be? Maybe he got shot again. Or was in jail? Or lying somewhere dead? She needed to concentrate on her own health, but her mind was focusing on all the bad things that could have happened to her father.

Just then, a nurse walked into her room. "Kim, you are going home today, and I need to make sure you can take care of yourself. I want you to explain, and demonstrate, how to check your blood sugar and give yourself insulin, like we went over yesterday."

Kim took the finger poker from the nurse.

"First I wipe off my finger, then I poke my finger and place the drop of blood on the test strip." Kim poked her finger and put the blood on the test strip. Then she placed the strip in the hand-held glucometer.

"Great job. Turn on the machine before you start so it is ready to go when you have the blood." The nurse picked up the glucometer and told Kim, "Your blood sugar is 96. You're on the right track. It's time to take your insulin, so I'll get that and your

230

breakfast. Here are your discharge papers. I want you to read them, and then give them to your caretaker when she arrives. I'll answer any questions you all have."

The nurse left the room, then returned five minutes later with the insulin pen and Kim's breakfast. Kim took the insulin pen, dialed it to six, then pressed the injector over her stomach and pressed the button. The pen quickly injected the medicine into her. It was so quick it startled her and she jumped. This wasn't so bad after all. It was quick and easy. The pen was dialed to the amount of insulin she needed, and when she depressed the button, the medicine entered her body. If she had to be honest, it hadn't hurt that bad.

A few minutes later, Allison and Kevin walked into the room. Kim handed her discharge papers to Allison. "Those are my discharge instructions."

Allison sat down in the chair next to the bed, and started reading the instructions, meticulously reading both sides.

"Are you feeling okay about checking your blood sugar and giving yourself a shot?" Allison asked.

"I am trying to be," Kim responded.

"I'll help. I have to go into work for a few hours, so Kevin is going to take you home for me," Allison explained.

"Okay," Kim responded.

The nurse walked back in the room. "Did you both get a chance to go over the discharge instructions?"

"Yes, I read through it. How soon does she need to see her doctor?" Allison asked.

"Sign here, please," the nurse said to Allison.

The nurse asked Kim to get dressed. Before

she left the room, she removed Kim's IV and said, "Call when you are ready to go."

Kim took the clothes Allison brought and went into the bathroom to shower and change. It felt good to shower after being stuck in that bed for days. When she dried herself off, she pulled on her pink cotton shirt and blue shorts.

"I'll see you at home, I have to get back to work," Allison said, as she headed for the door. "Kevin will take good care of you. And I've made lunch for you, so don't worry."

"Kim, I talked to your friend, Q," Kevin said. "Marissa is still in the hospital."

"Is she going to be alright?" Kim asked, realizing her brother had been silent all morning. He sat in the chair, alert and listening, but he hadn't said one word.

"I don't know much about it, but I thought I would offer to take you to see her," Kevin responded.

"Thanks, that would be great," Kim replied.

Twenty minutes later, they were pulling up to the Kaiser Hospital parking lot.

Kim texted Quaneisha. "I am here at the hospital. What room is Marissa in?"

"201, I'm here," Quaneisha texted back.

"I'm on my way up," Kim responded. Then she turned to Kevin. "Q's here. I'm going to head up. I won't stay long."

"I'll wait here for you," her brother replied.

Kim walked through the lobby, following the signs for the elevator, and then took it up to the second floor. Once on the right floor, she followed the arrow pointing toward rooms 201-215 and arrived at a big white door and sign that read "ICU. Please call for entry."

Kim picked up the phone and dialed the number. "I'm here to see the patient in room 201,

Marissa."

"Are you family?" the person asked.

"Yes," Kim answered, which wasn't really a lie. She felt like a sister to Marissa.

The door clicked and opened. As soon as Kim walked in she saw that tubes and wires were connected to her friend. Everything looked very serious, her heart started beating faster and faster. She walked up to the glass doors with the number 201. Quaneisha was sitting next to the bed, holding a hand. The hand was the only thing that resembled Marissa. The person in the bed's face was swollen, black and blue, and she had a long tube coming out of her mouth connecting to a machine. There were IV lines hooked up to pumps like Kim had in the hospital, but Marissa had an IV in each arm.

Kim walked up to Quaneisha and laid her hand on her shoulder. Quaneisha looked up at Kim with reddened eyes and a tear-streaked face.

"She got out of surgery late last night. She had internal bleeding from the fight with Carlos's friend. I don't think she even knew she was hurt so bad. I'm happy I called the ambulance. Now she's in a drug-induced coma," Quaneisha responded.

"I don't understand," Kim exclaimed. "Why did they put her in a coma?"

"Marissa kept pulling out her ventilator," Quaneisha explained.

"Will she be alright?" Kim asked.

"They don't know," Quaneisha responded, lowering her head and sobbing.

Kim hugged her friend, her body shaking from the grief.

"She has to be okay. They have to fix her," Kim said.

"They stopped the bleeding in surgery, and they're hoping to wake her up later tonight or early tomorrow. I have been talking to her because they say she can hear me."

Kim touched Marissa's hand. "Marissa, you have to fight so you can get better."

"I'm sorry I didn't come back to the hospital, but she was so sick. Kevin and his family were there for you and she had no one."

"Don't worry about me, Q. I'm glad you're here with her," Kim replied.

Kim's phone buzzed.

"Kim, I'm sorry to cut your visit short, but we have to go now. I'll bring you back later after you rest," Kevin texted.

"I have to go, but I'll be back," Kim said, squeezing Marissa's hand. "Marissa, we are here for you. Please come back to us."

Quaneisha walked Kim to the door, and they hugged each other, crying.

"You have to take care of yourself, too."

"I will. Where is your foster mom?" Kim asked.

"She had to go back to the doctor. She was here for a little while last night. I stayed the night. I don't want to leave her here alone," Quaneisha responded. "I have to leave for a few hours today because I have to go do my volunteer hours with Amy."

"Oh yeah, how is that going?" Kim asked.

"I am learning so much. I think I want to go to college and become a lawyer like Amy. It's been really cool to work there."

"I'll come back here this afternoon, and sit with her while you go to work," Kim responded, hugging her friend again.

She walked back to the elevator, tears falling down her face. Her own condition seemed unimportant now that she saw Marissa fighting for her life. While she had been worrying about poking herself, Marissa was near death. Kim walked through the lobby, wiping the tears that wouldn't stop. Kevin got out of the car and hugged her. "She looked so bad. Kids aren't supposed to be sick like this," Kim said.

"Come on, you have to get some rest, so I'll take you home. You have to take care of yourself or you're useless to your friends," Kevin said as he closed her car door.

They drove home in silence. Kim appeared worried as she looked out the window.

Chapter 32

Kim tossed and turned on her bed for two hours trying to rest. She kept seeing Marissa lying in the room smelling of alcohol, with the tubes coming out everywhere, unconscious, and pale. She looked so sick. Kim couldn't shake the uneasy feeling she felt leaving her friend at the hospital. She was resting like Allison and her brother requested, but she wanted to be with Marissa.

Kim eased out of the bed, grabbed her pink cell phone, and headed toward the kitchen. The house was quiet; everyone was out for the afternoon, at work and practice. They would all return for dinner at six-thirty.

Kim looked at the clock in the kitchen. She had three hours to spend with Marissa before dinner.

Her brother wouldn't be off until five-thirty, so she hoped Davion would give her a ride. Kim opened the door leading to the patio on the side of the house. Looking to the right, she could see Davion's car parked next to the curb of his house.

Kim walked over and rang his doorbell. Davion opened the door and smiled.

"You're home," he said, reaching for her hand and pulling her into an embrace.

Kim relaxed into his arms and hugged him back.

"Come in," he motioned for her to follow him. "Would you like a glass of water or a snack? My mother made some sandwiches."

Kim paused for a moment. Now that Davion mentioned food, she realized she was hungry. She had passed through the kitchen so fast; she hadn't looked for something to eat or the dose of her medicine Allison had left for her.

"I'll grab a bite at home; Allison left me something to eat," Kim replied.

"Let's walk back over to your place so you can eat then," Davion said. He grabbed the paper plate his mother had set down on the bar for him. "Mom, I am going to eat at Kim's house so she can take her medication."

"Alright, baby," his mom called out. "Welcome back home, Kim!"

Kim waved at his mother and followed Davion back out the front door. He held her hand as they walked toward the side patio.

"Let's eat out here. I'll grab my lunch and be right back," Kim said.

Davion set his plate on the patio table while Kim headed in the door that led into the kitchen, where she found a note and a covered plate on the table that read:

Here is your lunch. And I drew up your insulin dose that the doctor ordered before lunch.

Kim looked at the syringe pen and frowned. The nurse had showed her how to do the shot, but she wished she didn't have to. She wiped her stomach and squeezed a piece of skin up, held her breath, bit her lip, and plunged the tiny needle into her skin, injecting the five units of insulin. When the syringe was empty, she removed the needle and dropped it in the red bucket. The pinch she felt was over before she exhaled all the air in her lungs. She picked up her apple and ham sandwich, grabbed two bottles of water and headed back out to the patio.

"How's it going?" Davion asked.

Kim swallowed her bite of apple. "I'm still adjusting. Once they get my blood sugars better regulated, they're going to give me a pump that gives me insulin. Then I won't have to stick myself four times a day. I am looking forward to that," Kim responded, eating her sandwich and apple.

"I'm just happy to see you doing well. I know this is a big change for you, and big adjustment in your life," Davion said, as he finished eating his chips.

Kim nodded, salivating over the crispy Ruffles Davion was eating. Chips were one of her favorite snacks, and now she had to be careful of the amount of carbs she ate. But, she reminded herself, she didn't have time to be wallowing in her own self-pity. She had a sick friend who needed her attention.

"Will you drop me at the hospital?" Kim asked.

"Are you feeling okay?" Davion countered.

"Oh, I'm fine. I want to visit with Marissa for a while because Q has to go to her volunteer service and no one else will be there."

"Sure, get a snack and your things and I'll take you," Davion replied. He picked up his phone, sent his mother a message, and gathered the trash off the patio table.

Kim went inside and got her purse, along with a small pack with her blood sugar machine and insulin pens, just in case she needed more medicine. She had one hour before it was time to check her blood sugar. She called Allison to let her know Davion would be taking her to see Marissa and that she would be home for dinner. Davion was outside waiting for her in his car.

As soon as she got into the car, her phone rang. Kim answered, thinking Allison had called her back, "Hello?"

"Kim, this is Keith. I called you as soon as I could. Are you home from the hospital yet?" he asked.

"Yes, I got discharged today. Did you find out anything?" Kim asked. Hearing the apprehension in his voice quickened her heart. "Just tell me."

"First of all, he's okay," Keith replied.

Kim sighed; it didn't sound like he had good news for her. Keith had always given her the truth, even when it was painful. His reluctance to give her the information made her uneasy.

"Please just tell me."

"Your father is alive and well. He is in jail and that's why you haven't heard from him," Keith responded.

"What happened?" Kim asked.

"Apparently, he's being charged with several things: vehicular manslaughter and DUI. He had an accident and someone died. He's in jail waiting for his sentencing trial because he pleaded guilty to the charges," Keith said.

"How long will he be in jail?" Kim asked.

"He could get five to ten years in prison. It depends on what the judge decides. Can you stay where you are for now?" Keith asked.

"I don't know," Kim answered. "I might be too much for them to take care of now with my diabetes. What people would want to take on that burden?"

"Look, talk to them. I can tell them about your dad if you want me to," Keith responded.

"No, I'll do it. Thanks for telling me."

"I can talk to Tim's parents too, if you need me to. Tim is at football camp for two weeks and that's why he hasn't called you, but his mother is at home," Keith replied.

"Thanks, but not yet. I'll let you know what happens here."

Kim hung up the phone and stared out the window. She wanted her father to allow her to stay in California, but now that she was sick, she couldn't ask Kevin's parents to accept a teenager with an illness. She had become an expensive burden. Her father messed up again, and now Kim had to face the consequences. He lied and said he was done with alcohol, and now he was in jail paying for that lie. She wiped the tears as they fell.

The car pulled into the hospital parking lot. Davion remained silent through the whole conversation. He turned off the ignition and wiped her face with a Kleenex.

"What happened?"

Kim sat quietly, not trusting her voice to speak yet.

"Don't count out Kevin's parents. They are great people. Allison will not put you out. She's not that type of person," Davion said.

Kim wiped the tears, "I know, but I don't want to be a burden either."

"All kids are burdens at one time or another. It's the life of a parent; let them make the call. I bet they will surprise you," Davion responded. "You could always come live in my room. It wouldn't be a burden to me." He smiled and squeezed her hand.

Kim smiled and got out of the car. "You can leave me, I'll catch the bus or call Kevin for a ride home," Kim replied.

"I'll wait, if you don't mind," Davion said.

"Come on in with me then," Kim answered.

They walked into the hospital lobby, heading for the elevator. The doors opened to the second floor, and they called to gain entry to the ICU. When Kim walked into her room, Marissa was still lying there with her eyes closed. Kim sat down and touched her friend's swollen fingers. Davion sat down next to Kim.

"They say people can hear you when they are in a coma," Kim said.

"I've heard that before on a movie I was watching," Davion replied. "Tell us a story."

Kim focused on Marissa swollen fingers. "I've never told you about my home in Texas. It was a small town where everyone knows everybody. That is good and bad. Good, because when I lost my mother a few years ago, my friends' parents fed me and opened their homes when I needed a place to hang out. Bad, because there are no secrets in our neighborhood, news spreads like a wildfire," Kim explained. She sighed and continued talking, "My father started drinking more and more when my mother died. He lost his job and stopped paying the bills. My neighbor Tim's parents gave us water. My friend Keith was the person who helped me look for Kevin when he left to come live with his parents here. I thought he had run away from home, but instead, he had run to a real home."

Davion got up and pulled Kim out of the chair into his lap and wrapped his arm around her, remaining quiet as she told her story.

"Oh yeah, I forgot. I found out my parents had adopted me and my brother. See, Kevin found his real parents, so his family was reunited, but I have lost the parents who gave birth to me, along with the ones who promised to love and care for me when my parents could not," Kim continued. "You see, my father is not perfect, but he does love me. I know he is unable to care for me when he's drinking, but Kevin and my father are all I have left."

"Sometimes parents make mistakes. Hopefully, your father will get himself together one day. Meanwhile, he has to want the best for you."

"Well, he didn't consider me when he got behind the wheel drinking, and now he will have to pay for his bad judgment—and I will too."

"Give Kevin's parents a chance. I'm sure they will want you to stay there."

"We'll see," Kim responded.

The nurse walked into the room, "Do you know the patient's parents?"

"Her foster mother," Kim replied.

"We need to reach her," the nurse responded.

"Is Marissa alright?" Kim asked.

"I'm afraid I can't give out any information, it violates her rights," the nurse said. "Please tell her sister to tell their mother to get in touch with us. We have been trying to reach her," the nurse said as she left the room.

Kim looked over at her friend, machines beeping and tubes coming out of her body, and wondered if Marissa would ever be the same dancing, smiling girl she met at the park earlier in the summer.

"Kim, it's six. We should leave so that you'll be home in time for dinner," Davion said.

Kim nodded, but she felt a great reluctance to leave her friend's side.

"Marissa, rest now and get better. I will always have your back. See you tomorrow," Kim whispered, bending down and kissing her friend's cold cheek. Kim followed Davion out of the room, glancing back at the body of her friend. "Thanks again. This meant the world to me."

"You've become really special to me." Davion stopped as they walked out the hospital door. "That's why I asked you to be my girlfriend."

"Yes," Kim replied.

"Huh?" Davion looked puzzled.

"The answer to your question is, yes. I wanna be your girlfriend."

"I'm juiced," Davion shouted with his hands in the air and jumping like a boxer who'd just scored a knockout. He hugged her, gave her a soft kiss on the lips, and held her hand as they walked toward his car.

When she and Davion were just about back at Davion's car, Kim stopped and turned back toward the hospital. She saw Marissa's foster mom walking briskly toward the entrance. Something was wrong. The nurse had asked Kim about contacting Marissa's family, and now Miss Ella was here.

Kim's legs started moving before her mind registered where it was headed. She had to get back to Marissa. Something wasn't right. Footsteps followed her quick pace through the entrance and up the elevator.

When Kim got to the ICU, Marissa's foster mom was talking to the doctor.

"I give my consent for the surgery," Miss Ella said.

Davion hugged Kim close. She was shaking, and she turned into him, letting his strength support her. Her friend must've been in danger if they wanted to operate right then. It had not seemed so bad when Kim first saw Marissa in that park. Her friend was awake and talking. What had gone so wrong that she needed surgery again?

"We are taking her now. She had some internal bleeding we need to fix," the doctor said. "Julie, I want her in the OR in ten minutes. The team will be ready."

"I'll call the transport team," Nurse Julie replied.

"Please help her," Kim told the retreating doctor.

"I'll do my best," the doctor replied.

"The waiting room for surgery is down the hall on the right. You guys can wait there," Julie informed the small group.

They all turned and headed toward the waiting room. Davion held Kim's hand, squeezing it as they walked. She sat down across from Miss Ella. Her family had failed Marissa when she needed them the most. She turned to the gang for love, when she felt alone. But she hadn't found anything there except more pain.

Quaneisha walked through the door, breathless. "I came as fast as I could. How is she?" she asked, sitting on the other side of Kim.

"She is in surgery; they said she was having difficulty breathing and maybe she was bleeding internally," the foster mother answered.

While they all waited to learn the results of the surgery, Kim bowed her head and prayed Marissa would be okay. She thought about the days her mother had been home in pain and sick. Those were some dark days.

The sadness brought out anger in her mother's family. They blamed her father for her mother's death. Kim was angry too; angry that her mom died, but it hadn't helped. The anger was selfish; her mother didn't want to die. The cancer killed her.

Kim knew this, but she couldn't help feeling angry. Kim still wished she could go back in time and change the outcome. Her life had fallen apart on the day her mother died. "I can't lose anyone else," Kim said, hugging herself and slowly rocking back and forth. "Please let her be ok."

When the doctor walked into the room, everyone converged on him like a pack of hungry wolves.

"Is she alright?" Quaneisha asked.

Kim squeezed her hand and Davion squeezed Kim's other hand. Barely breathing, they all awaited the doctor's answer. The doctor neutral facial expression gave no answers.

He crossed his hands in front of his body and began speaking.

"We did everything we could, but your daughter had a pulmonary embolus, a clot went to her heart, and we lost her on the table. We tried to revive her, but we couldn't get her heart to start working again. She had an enlarged heart and it couldn't take the stress. I am so very sorry," he informed them. "A social worker is on her way to help you all get through this."

Kim couldn't fill the hole that started to form inside. She couldn't see through the pain and tears. Death had found her again. She wanted to escape the pain. Warm hands were hugging her on both sides.

Quaneisha sobbed. Kim squeezed her. Davion had his arms around her, too. Kim kept seeing her mother lying in the bed looking around the room one last time before she took her last breath.

Kim held herself, tears falling down her face. "God has a plan, and he doesn't give us more than we can handle. He has Marissa now," Miss Ella said, as she started rocking side to side and fanning herself.

"Maybe you should sit down," Quaneisha

said, reaching to help her foster mother.

The social worker came in the room and started talking to Miss Ella and Quaneisha.

"We should go, Kim. You've had a stressful week," Davion said.

Kim knew he was right, but she didn't want to leave her friend. She felt so helpless. Nothing she'd done had saved Marissa. She called and texted, warning her about the danger involved with gangs. Maybe there was something else she could have done to get her friend to stay away from that gang.

"If I only tried harder," Kim said in between sobs.

"You can't make other people's decisions for them. You gave her the information and she made the choice. I wish things had turned out differently, but my grandmother always says, 'Are you ready to live with the consequences of your actions?'" Davion told Kim firmly.

He was so painfully right that Kim wondered how she was lucky enough to have him around.

She nodded her head and allowed him to lead her toward the door. "Just a second," Kim said to Davion. She ran over to Quaneisha and hugged her. "Call me later, Q."

"She would want you to take care of yourself, too," Davion said as they left the hospital and walked toward his car. "When I lost my dad, I thought my world ended, but it helped to remember he was not in pain anymore. He was at peace, and Marissa is at peace now. You have to honor her by living a good life."

"How did you get so wise?" Kim asked.

"My grandmother was the wise one. When I was younger, she made me come over every Sunday to help in her garden. She would tell me stories about my dad, and then we would plant some vegetables.

246

She said that garden was to honor my dad; we planted all his favorites. Later she called it, our healing garden," Davion replied.

"Did it help?" Kim asked.

Davion turned onto Noeline Avenue and headed down the hill, "Yes, she was right. It felt better to honor his memory than mourn his loss. It helped my mother too. We were lucky to have my grandmother."

"It was hard when I lost my mom. Everyone was so busy grieving that no one honored her life. I want to honor both my mother and Marissa," Kim said.

Davion had been her rock through this terrible event. He was so right; you had to honor the lives of the family and friends you lost. Kim missed her mother tremendously, and she knew now that her mother hadn't chosen to leave her. Honor her? She could learn to sew. She remembered all the clothes Maggie made for her.

They pulled up in front of Kim's house.

"Call me after dinner," Davion said, as Kim got out of the car. Kim nodded her head, and walked up the drive, tears still dripping down her chin.

Chapter 33

When Kim walked into the kitchen, everyone was sitting at the table. She didn't want to eat. Her appetite was gone. She dropped her head and mumbled a hello to the family. Allison was the first person out of her chair. She walked over to Kim and hugged her. Kim's body shook as she let the grief pour out of her.

Allison lifted her chin. "Tell me what happened."

"Marissa died," she managed to say between sobs.

"I'm so sorry," Allison said. Allison took her by the hand and led her to the bathroom. She washed her face, gently. Then she took her to her room. "You have had a lot of grief in your young life. I want you to remember the good times you had with your friend. I'm here to help you get through this."

"Thank you," Kim said, taking a deep breath.

"I know you are not hungry, but you have to eat. You have to take care of yourself. Will you come back to the table with me?" Allison asked.

Kim knew Allison was right. She did not want to end up back in the hospital. Honoring her friend's memory meant she had to live her life. Her diabetes demanded she eat regular meals. She would force something down her stomach.

"I'll come," Kim replied.

"I have your insulin ready for you. Here, let me give it to you," Allison said. Kim raised her shirt and allowed Allison to give her the injection. "Wash up and I will meet you at the table."

Kim lowered her shirt, washed her face and hands, and headed back to the dining room for dinner. She sat next to Kevin, who reached up and held her hand, mouthing he was sorry. Kim heard Robert praying, thanking God for many blessings he had received. And he asked that he take care of Marissa, and then everyone said, "Amen."

The food smelled delicious, it looked like a feast. There was smothered cabbage, grilled pork chops, and rice with brown gravy. Kim passed the food as she was asked to and served herself a small portion of each item, except for the gravy. The food was warm and tasty, but Kim felt like a robot going through the motions. She forced herself to eat bite after bite, until her stomach started to protest. Placing her fork down, she asked to be excused.

"Won't you please stay with us at the table a little longer?" Allison requested, squeezing her husband's hand.

Kim nodded, even though she wanted to go to her room and bury her head in a pillow and cry. No one understood the pain she was going through.

She sat there trying to be pleasant, but her insides were shredding, and the food felt like lead on the bottom of her stomach. If she sat here another minute she would start screaming. Robert was talking, but Kim couldn't understand him

"We wanted to talk to you," Robert said. "This summer has been like a rollercoaster for you. You have an extraordinary devotion to your friends, and they are very lucky to have you."

"Thank you," Kim acknowledged.

"I hope you had some fun this summer."

Kim nodded. She was afraid her voice would crack if she spoke. Fun was an understatement. She could just be a kid here. They had provided everything a kid could ever want. That's why the idea of leaving hurt so badly.

"We wanted to let you know you've touched our family, too. Your dedication and strength are admirable. We had a family meeting, and Allison and I would like to have you live with us permanently. We feel like you're already a part of the family," Robert informed her. "You see, when we got information on Kevin, they also told us about you. When we made the decision to try to get him back, we included you in that package."

"We wanted both of you. When Kevin came, we still held out hope that you would come too. It was a little more difficult with you because your father didn't want to allow it," Allison chimed in.

Kim's eyes got bigger and glossy as Robert and Allison continued speaking. This had to be a dream.

"We asked our lawyer to find your father, and she found him in jail awaiting trial. He has agreed, after talking to Kevin, to sign over temporary custody to us if we allowed you to speak with him. He is calling at eight to talk to you. We want to know if you would like to stay with us and become a part of our family," Robert said.

Kevin chimed in, "Kim, I remember the beginning of the summer you asked if I could forgive Francis and I said no. Well watching you sacrifice for your friends and hold your head high to face this diabetes, I decided to try and forgive him. He apologized to me, and I told him if he loved you, he had to allow my parents the chance to help you through this disease. We all want you to stay."

Julian nodded and Marcus smiled and nodded his head.

Kim searched each face at the table, seeing the honesty and truth in their statements, but one person remained silent through this whole discussion. Could she live permanently in a room with Andrea? They had had a rough summer. She had been nice to Kim in the hospital, but would that truce hold? She looked at Andrea and tried to read her silence.

"I'm in too. Just keep your side of the room neat," Andrea replied.

"Yeah, okay," Kim responded back.

Maybe she and Andrea had finally turned a corner to a real friendship and would be able to move towards a sister relationship. Kim could be a faithful servant in her court, but it had taken a whole summer for Andrea to allow her into her realm.

"I'm serious. Don't touch any of my stuff, or we will have a problem," Andrea fired back.

"Andrea, behave!" Allison chastised.

"I'm just setting some boundaries for my new sister," Andrea replied.

"Boundaries work both ways and I will set them," Allison responded with finality.

Kim smiled. That was the old Andrea, the familiar Andrea. But at least she was trying.

These people wanted to become her new

family for better or worse. Kim felt warmth and joy fill her entire body. The hole in heart felt like it was mending. Her mother would have been happy.

Kim's thoughts were interrupted by the phone ringing. "I'll get it."

"It's okay to accept the collect call," Robert informed her.

"Collect call from Parris County Correction facility, inmate Francis," the recording said. "Press one to accept the call or two to end this call."

Kim pressed one and waited for the call to be connected. She felt conflicted; she should be happy, but it felt sad to get what you want because your father was in jail. She wanted him to be getting his act together, not rotting in a cell. Tragedy had swept through their family and left a path of destruction. Her father had lost his wife, job, house, and kids. He needed to catch a break and start a new life.

"Hey, baby girl," Francis said, sounding closer to the dad she knew and loved. His voice resonated love and strength. "I know you are sad, but don't you be sad for me. I am going to be all right. I need you to take care of yourself. You hear me?"

"Yes, I hear you," Kim replied, taking the phone into the family room to have a little more privacy. "I'm so sorry that you're in jail."

"Yeah, well I'm not. Something about being confined has given me some clarity. I've been here for three weeks, and my body is feeling great. I think about you kids and your mom, and I know she would be happy about where you guys are. You're making us both proud, so don't be sorry," Francis replied. "I need you to go to college and follow your dreams. Remember when you told me you wanted to become a doctor. Well, I need you to work hard and become that doctor."

"I will," Kim said through tears.

"I'm so ashamed of my mistakes, Kim. I just hope you will forgive me. Tell Kevin I'm sorry, too, and he was right. It's time to start honoring Maggie's memory and making better decisions. You both deserved better from me. Baby girl, I love you and I want you to write me and send me pictures so I will be able to witness your triumphs. You hear me?"

"I'll write. I promise," Kim replied.

"They told me about your diabetes. My father had diabetes and he didn't eat what he was supposed to or do what his doctors told him to do. He lost a foot and his life. I need you to listen to those doctors and do what they say, okay?"

"Okay," Kim said.

"It would break my heart to lose you, so I want your health and education to be your number one priority. When I get out, I will be someone you can be proud of again. Now my time is up. I have to get off the phone. Tell Robert I signed the papers this morning, and he better take care of my baby. Tell him now so I can hear it."

"Robert," Kim said, walking back into the kitchen, "my father said he signed the papers and to please take care of me," Kim repeated.

"We will," Allison and Robert replied in unison. "Tell him he may call you once a month collect," Robert replied.

"They said they would and that you may call once a month, collect," Kim repeated.

"Thank them. I will talk to you next month then. I love you," her father said.

"I love you, too," Kim replied, as she hung up the phone. This was bittersweet. She was giving up one family for another. She wanted them both, but it was not in the cards. She had lost too many people in her life. She thought about her friend Marissa and realized you had to make each moment count. Kim wiped her tear-streaked face and walked back to the table to finish her dinner.

"Kim, we are so happy you're staying with us. Most of the times kids don't get to pick their families, they are stuck with whatever family ties they are born with. But you have been blessed to have enriched two family lines. Welcome!" Allison responded.

"When I lost my mother, I thought my family ties were gone and lost forever. When Kevin left and my father starting drinking, I dreamed of having a family again. Your home has exceeded my dreams and thank you for your invitation to live here," Kim replied.

Kevin stood and walked around to his sister and hugged her. Allison and Robert followed Kevin, Julian and Marcus were next, and then Andrea came around the table and hugged Kim. Her mother Maggie would be happy, and Kim would work hard to make both of her families proud. Kim found her home.

www.ingramcontent.com/pod-product-compliance
Lightning Source LLC
Chambersburg PA
CBHW022001170626
46808CB00001B/240